GW01406650

Shadows Of The Fireflies

Fireflies Of The Heart, Volume 2

Night Intruder

Published by Night Intruder, 2024.

This is a work of fiction. Similarities to real people, places, or events are entirely coincidental.

SHADOWS OF THE FIREFLIES

First edition. October 9, 2024.

Copyright © 2024 Night Intruder.

ISBN: 979-8227544018

Written by Night Intruder.

Table of Contents

To those who wander through the shadows,

And to those who light the way.

This is for the dreamers, the fighters,

And the ones who find strength in the dark.

For every firefly that guides you home.

Chapter 1: Whispers in the Dark

The forest was behind her, but its presence lingered like a shadow in her mind. The firefly's light had flickered out, and with it, the fragile sense of safety she had clung to. The road stretched ahead, but Evelyn couldn't shake the feeling that it wasn't over—that the forest's reach extended far beyond its twisted trees.

Her breath came In ragged gasps as she stumbled forward, each step heavier than the last. The night was unnaturally quiet. No crickets, no wind. Only the silence—and the occasional whisper that echoed faintly in her mind.

"Evelyn..."

She stopped, her heart skipping a beat. The voice was soft, almost drowned out by the pounding of her pulse, but it was there. She could feel it. Him. Her lost love. The one she had thought was trapped in the forest.

But now she knew the terrible truth. He wasn't just trapped—he was part of it. The forest had claimed him, twisted him, and now it was trying to claim her too.

She shook her head, trying to clear the fog of exhaustion and fear that clouded her thoughts. The road stretched on, endless and desolate. Every step felt like she was sinking deeper into quicksand, but she kept moving. She had to. There was no going back.

The air was thick with moisture, the kind that clung to her skin and made her feel like she was being watched. Her clothes stuck to her body, cold and damp, but she barely noticed. All she could think about was getting away, putting as much distance between herself and the forest as possible.

But the forest had other plans.

The first sign was the wind. It came out of nowhere, a sudden gust that sent a chill racing down her spine. The leaves rustled in the trees above her, their whispers blending with the faint voice in her mind. She froze, her breath catching in her throat.

The road was empty, but she could feel it—the presence, creeping closer, just out of sight. It was watching her. Waiting.

"You can't escape..."

The voice was louder this time, more insistent. It came from everywhere and nowhere at once, as though the very air around her was whispering her name. Her pulse quickened, her breath coming in short, panicked gasps.

Evelyn turned, her eyes scanning the darkness, but there was nothing. Just the road, the trees, and the oppressive weight of the night pressing down on her. She forced herself to take a step forward, then another. She had to keep moving.

But the whispers followed.

The wind picked up, howling through the trees like a wounded animal. The fireflies—those faint, flickering lights that had once guided her—were gone, swallowed by the darkness. She was alone, and the forest wasn't going to let her go.

The road beneath her feet began to crack, the pavement splitting like brittle bones. Evelyn stumbled, her heart racing as the ground trembled. She reached out to steady herself, but there was nothing to grab hold of. The earth was shifting, pulling her back toward the forest.

"Come back to me..."

His voice. The one she had loved, the one she had lost. But it wasn't him anymore. It couldn't be. The forest had claimed him, twisted him into something dark, something evil. And now it was trying to claim her too.

The ground gave way beneath her, a jagged fissure splitting the road in two. She screamed, her body falling into the darkness, the cold earth swallowing her whole.

But just as quickly as it had come, the ground solidified, trapping her ankle in its grip. She gasped, her hands clawing at the pavement as she struggled to free herself. The whispers grew louder, more insistent, their voices blending into a cacophony of sound that drowned out her own thoughts.

"You belong to the forest... You can't escape..."

Her pulse pounded in her ears as she yanked her leg free, her body trembling with fear and exhaustion. She stumbled forward, her breath coming in ragged gasps, but the road seemed to stretch on forever, twisting and warping in the darkness. There was no escape. The forest had let her go, but its grasp was still strong, pulling her back, pulling her down.

Evelyn fell to her knees, her hands trembling as she pressed them against the cold, cracked pavement. The fireflies were gone. The road was gone. The whispers were all that remained, echoing through the night like a cruel reminder that she would never be free.

"Come back..."

The voice was right behind her now, so close she could feel its breath on her neck. She spun around, her heart racing, but there was nothing. Only the darkness. Only the whispers.

Tears filled her eyes as the weight of the forest settled over her like a heavy shroud. She had escaped, but it had followed her. It was inside her now, creeping through her thoughts, twisting her memories, turning everything she had known into a nightmare.

And then she saw it—a faint, flickering light in the distance. A firefly.

Her breath hitched, her pulse quickening as the light grew brighter, cutting through the darkness like a beacon. It wasn't like the other fireflies. This one was different. It felt... alive.

Evelyn staggered to her feet, her body trembling as she took a step toward the light. The whispers faltered, just for a moment, and in that moment, she knew—this wasn't the end.

It was only the beginning.

Chapter 2: The Hunt Begins

The night had turned colder, the air thick with a sense of dread, suffocating in its stillness. Evelyn had escaped the forest, or so she thought, but the firefly's light had long since flickered out, leaving her in near darkness. She felt the forest breathing, alive and watching her, as though Its ancient evil had stretched out beyond its borders, reaching for her with invisible claws.

Her legs burned from running, and her breath came in shallow, panicked gasps. Each step felt heavier, as though the weight of the earth itself was dragging her down, pulling her back toward the nightmare she had just left behind.

But the silence unnerved her most. No wind stirred the leaves, no insects buzzed in the night air—just the oppressive quiet, broken only by the occasional crackle of distant branches snapping. A sound that wasn't random, but deliberate. Something was moving, closing in.

A sharp crack broke the silence—a branch snapping underfoot, but not hers.

Evelyn froze, her heart pounding in her ears. She turned slowly, her breath caught in her throat as her eyes scanned the darkness behind her. The road stretched back into a black, endless void, the trees barely visible beneath the thick mist that clung to the earth like a living thing.

But she wasn't alone.

The firefly's faint flicker had been her only guide, but now, it was gone, swallowed by the encroaching shadows. The unease in her chest tightened into panic. She reached into her pocket, feeling for the stone that had once pulsed with warmth, a lifeline in the forest's grip. But it too was cold, its power drained.

A low, guttural growl rippled through the air, vibrating deep in her bones. The sound sent a jolt of terror through her body, her heart skipping a beat. She knew that growl. It wasn't human. And it wasn't far.

Her pulse quickened, her hands shaking as the growl echoed again, louder this time, more menacing. She could feel it, the presence lurking just beyond the edge of the fog, watching her, waiting for the right moment to strike.

A pair of glowing eyes appeared in the darkness, shining like two lanterns against the black. Her stomach twisted in fear, her body locking in place. The creature was huge, its silhouette barely visible as it moved between the trees, its eyes glowing with unnatural light.

The forest had sent It for her.

The creature stepped out of the fog, its massive form coming into view. It was a wolf—or what had once been a wolf. But this thing was no ordinary animal. Its fur was matted and torn, patches of flesh hanging loose like ragged cloth. Its teeth gleamed under the faint moonlight, sharp and jagged, glistening with saliva. But it was the eyes—those glowing, unblinking eyes—that filled Evelyn with a terror she couldn't escape. Those eyes were not of this world. They belonged to the forest.

It growled again, the sound vibrating through the air, low and feral. The forest had twisted it into something monstrous, and now it was hunting her.

Evelyn took a step back, her legs trembling beneath her, but she couldn't run. The road behind her was nothing but darkness and fog. There was no escape. The forest was alive, and it wanted her.

The beast's snarl grew louder, and with a sudden burst of speed, it lunged at her, its massive body hurtling through the air. Evelyn screamed, her body moving on instinct as she threw herself to the side.

The creature's claws grazed her arm, tearing through her shirt, and she hit the ground hard, her breath knocked from her lungs.

The beast let out a deafening roar, its eyes glowing brighter as it turned to face her. It paced slowly, like a predator toying with its prey, savoring the fear it could smell on her skin. It crouched low, muscles tensing, preparing for another strike.

Evelyn scrambled to her feet, her body shaking with exhaustion and fear. Her mind raced, but there was no plan. There was nothing she could do. She was unarmed, and the firefly's light—her only hope—was gone.

The creature lunged again, Its jaws snapping just inches from her face, and Evelyn barely managed to roll out of the way. She hit the ground again, her body aching from the Impact, but there was no time to feel the pain.

The forest had sent this beast for her, and it wouldn't stop until it had her.

Her heart pounded in her chest, her breath coming in short, shallow gasps as the creature stalked toward her. Its eyes locked on her, glowing with a hunger that chilled her to the core.

Then, out of nowhere, a sharp whistle cut through the air, startling the beast. It stopped, its head snapping toward the sound, its ears twitching in confusion.

"Get down!" a voice shouted from the darkness.

Evelyn didn't think—she dropped to the ground just as something sharp and silver shot past her, slicing through the air with deadly precision. The creature let out a furious snarl, but it was too late. The silver blade struck its side, sinking deep into its flesh. The beast howled in pain, thrashing wildly as it tried to free itself.

A figure emerged from the shadows, moving with speed and precision, another blade in hand. The figure was tall, strong, and moved with a grace that Evelyn could only describe as predatory. With a single, swift movement, the figure plunged the second blade into the creature's neck, silencing it for good.

The beast collapsed to the ground with a heavy thud, its glowing eyes fading into darkness.

Evelyn stared in disbelief as the figure stood over the fallen creature, breathing heavily. The stranger wiped the blade clean on the creature's fur before turning to face her.

"You okay?" the voice asked.

It was a woman, tall and strong, her face sharp and determined, eyes filled with a fierce resolve. She extended a hand to Evelyn, pulling her to her feet.

Before Evelyn could respond, another figure stepped out of the shadows—a man, his expression equally intense, a bow slung across his back.

"She's not safe here," the man said, his voice low and urgent. "The forest won't stop with this one. We need to move."

Evelyn's pulse raced as she looked between the two strangers. Her mind was spinning, her body trembling with exhaustion and fear, but there was no time for questions.

"Who are you?" she asked, her voice barely above a whisper.

The woman gave her a sharp nod. "Allies," she said simply. "And you're in more danger than you realize."

The man glanced at the fallen creature, his expression grim. "This is only the beginning," he said. "The forest is hunting you now. It won't stop."

Evelyn swallowed hard, her body shaking as the reality of the situation sank in. The forest wasn't done with her. It had let her go, but only because it had more in store for her. More creatures. More terror.

The woman stepped forward, her eyes scanning the trees. "We need to go," she said. "Now."

Without another word, she turned and began walking down the road, her steps quick and purposeful. The man followed closely behind, his eyes never leaving the trees.

Evelyn hesitated for a moment, her body trembling with fear and exhaustion. She didn't know who these people were or why they were helping her, but she had no choice. She couldn't face the forest alone.

With a deep breath, she followed them into the night, the whispers of the forest echoing in her mind.

The worst was yet to come.

Chapter 3: Allies in the Shadows

The wind had shifted, carrying with it the damp scent of moss and earth. The two strangers moved swiftly ahead, their steps confident and assured, as though they knew these cursed woods better than anyone. The man, silent but watchful, scanned the trees as they walked, while the woman led with purposeful strides, her blades gleaming faintly under the pale moonlight.

Evelyn struggled to keep up, her legs heavy with exhaustion, her mind clouded by the terrifying events of the night. Her breath came in ragged gasps, and though her body screamed for rest, she couldn't stop. Not now. Not when the forest was hunting her.

"Who are you?" Evelyn finally asked, her voice hoarse from the cold night air. She had been trailing behind them for what felt like hours, but now that the immediate threat had passed, she needed answers.

The woman glanced over her shoulder, her sharp features softened slightly by the moonlight. "Names aren't important right now," she said curtly. "What matters is getting you out of here alive."

Evelyn swallowed hard, her eyes narrowing as she studied the two strangers. They moved with precision, their steps quiet, calculated. They weren't ordinary people. They knew the forest—its dangers, its secrets. But that only raised more questions.

"Why are you helping me?" Evelyn asked, her voice tinged with suspicion.

The man, who had been silent until now, turned his head slightly, his gaze meeting hers for the first time. His face was stern, weathered by years of experience, but there was something in his eyes—something that hinted at a deeper connection to the horrors she was facing.

"Because the forest is waking up," he said, his voice low, almost a whisper. "And you're part of it now."

A chill ran down Evelyn's spine, her heart skipping a beat. She wasn't sure what he meant, but the weight of his words hung in the air like a dark omen.

The woman slowed her pace, allowing Evelyn to catch up. "Look," she said, her tone softening slightly, "you've seen what the forest is capable of. You've seen the creatures it controls, the way it twists and bends the world to its will. We're here to make sure you don't fall victim to it."

Evelyn's pulse quickened as her mind raced. "But... why me? Why is the forest after me?"

The woman exchanged a glance with the man, their silent communication unsettling. There was something they weren't telling her.

The man spoke again, his voice steady but grave. "The forest doesn't just target anyone. It chooses people—people who are connected to it, whether they know it or not."

Evelyn frowned, confusion twisting in her chest. "Connected? What are you talking about? I came here to find someone, but... I'm not connected to this place."

The woman stopped walking, turning to face Evelyn fully. Her eyes bore into her, as though she were searching for something beneath the surface. "That's where you're wrong," she said quietly. "You're connected to this forest in ways you can't even begin to understand. And so is the person you came here for."

Evelyn's heart pounded in her chest as the realization sank in. Her lost love—the man she had thought was trapped, the man she had believed she could save—was part of this. Part of the forest. Part of the curse.

"But... he's not—" Evelyn's voice broke, her mind reeling as the pieces began to fall into place.

The woman's expression softened, but there was a sadness in her eyes that told Evelyn everything she needed to know. "He's gone, Evelyn. The forest has him now."

A wave of grief crashed over her, threatening to pull her under. She had come here to find him, to save him, but he was already lost. The forest had twisted him, claimed him as its own. And now it was coming for her.

"We don't have time for this," the man interrupted, his voice sharp. "We need to keep moving before the next wave hits."

The woman nodded, her gaze lingering on Evelyn for a moment before turning away. "We'll explain more when we're safe," she said over her shoulder. "But for now, you need to trust us."

Evelyn's mind spun with questions, but there was no time to ask them. The air had changed again, growing heavier, thicker with the scent of decay. Something was coming.

The three of them moved swiftly through the trees, their steps almost soundless against the damp earth. But Evelyn couldn't shake the feeling that they were being followed, that the forest's eyes were still on her, watching her every move.

The firefly's light had returned, faint but flickering ahead of them like a distant beacon. But it wasn't the comforting light it had once been. Now it felt like a warning.

As they walked, Evelyn noticed something strange about the trees. They seemed... closer, more twisted, their branches reaching down like skeletal hands, as though they were alive. The shadows between the trees were darker, deeper, and every now and then, she thought she saw movement—something lurking just out of sight.

"Stay close," the woman whispered, her hand gripping the hilt of her blade.

Evelyn's heart raced, her eyes darting around as the shadows shifted and moved. The whispers had returned, soft at first, but growing louder with every step.

"Evelyn..."

She froze, her breath catching in her throat. That voice. It was his voice. The man she had loved, the man she had lost. The man who had become part of the forest.

"Don't listen to it," the man said sharply, his eyes scanning the trees. "The forest uses the voices of the lost to lure you in. It's not him."

But the whispers grew louder, more insistent.

"Evelyn... come back to me..."

Her pulse quickened, her mind racing as the shadows twisted around her. She could feel it—the pull of the forest, the way it reached for her, called to her. It wanted her. And deep down, part of her wanted to go back. Part of her wanted to find him.

The woman stepped closer, her hand resting on Evelyn's shoulder. "Focus," she said quietly. "Don't let it take you."

Evelyn nodded, forcing herself to take a deep breath. But the whispers were relentless, echoing through her mind, twisting her thoughts.

And then, out of the corner of her eye, she saw it.

A figure, standing between the trees, barely visible in the darkness. Its outline was faint, but she knew that shape. She knew that face.

It was him.

"Evelyn..." the voice called again, softer this time, more pleading. "Come back to me..."

Her body moved on its own, her feet carrying her toward the figure before she even realized what was happening. The firefly's light flickered wildly, as though trying to warn her, but she couldn't stop.

"Evelyn, no!" the woman shouted, grabbing her arm and yanking her back.

The figure disappeared, melting into the shadows as quickly as it had appeared. The whispers faded, replaced by the rustling of leaves and the distant sound of growling—more creatures, coming closer.

Evelyn's heart pounded in her chest, her breath coming in short, panicked gasps. She had almost lost herself. Almost given in to the forest's pull.

"We need to move," the man said urgently, his bow already drawn. "Now."

The woman nodded, her grip tightening on her blade. "Stick together," she said, her voice steady. "The forest is trying to break you. Don't let it."

Evelyn swallowed hard, her mind still reeling from the vision she had seen. Was it real? Was he still out there, somewhere in the shadows? Or was it just another trick of the forest, another way to lure her back?

She didn't know. And that terrified her more than anything.

As they moved deeper into the forest, the air grew colder, the shadows longer. The firefly's light flickered ahead of them, its glow dimming with every step. And Evelyn knew, without a doubt, that the forest was far from finished with her.

The hunt had only just begun.

Chapter 4: Beneath the Surface

The further they walked, the more Evelyn felt the forest closing in around them. The air was thick with moisture, every breath heavier than the last. The trees seemed alive, twisting and contorting into unnatural shapes as if they were leaning in to watch her, their gnarled branches reaching out like skeletal hands.

It wasn't just the whispers anymore. The ground beneath her feet felt wrong, almost as though it was shifting, waiting for her to misstep. The firefly's faint light, which had once been her guide, now flickered erratically, barely illuminating the path ahead.

The man with the bow, always a step ahead, turned sharply and held up his hand, signaling them to stop. Evelyn could barely make out his face in the dim light, but she could see the tension in his posture. He was listening, sensing something she couldn't.

"What is it?" Evelyn whispered, her voice barely audible over the pounding of her heart.

The man didn't answer right away. His eyes were locked on something in the distance, his fingers flexing around the bowstring as if ready to strike.

The woman, her hand gripping her blade, narrowed her eyes. "We're not alone," she muttered, her voice tight.

Evelyn's pulse quickened. These two strangers had saved her, but they hadn't told her who they were, or why they were risking their lives for her. They moved through the forest like they knew it intimately—knew its secrets, its dangers—but something about them remained a mystery.

The ground trembled beneath her feet, sending a jolt of fear through her body. The earth beneath them began to shake, the ground splitting in jagged cracks that snaked across the path.

"What's happening?" Evelyn asked, her voice trembling.

The man's grip tightened on his bow. "The forest," he said, his voice low and steady, "it's shifting."

Before Evelyn could process his words, the ground erupted, and a massive sinkhole opened up right in front of them. The earth gave way, collapsing in on itself with a deafening roar, sending rocks and debris tumbling into the abyss below.

Evelyn stumbled backward, barely managing to stay on her feet as the sinkhole swallowed the path ahead. She stared in disbelief as the ground continued to collapse, the trees groaning as their roots were torn from the earth.

"What is that?" Evelyn gasped, her voice barely audible over the sound of the earth crumbling.

The woman, her expression hardened, glanced at the man. "More of the forest's games," she said. "It won't stop until it gets what it wants."

The ground trembled again, and this time, it wasn't just the earth that moved. A low growl echoed from the sinkhole, deep and guttural, followed by the sound of something scraping against the rocks.

Evelyn's breath hitched as a massive shape emerged from the darkness below, its form hidden by the shadows, but its presence unmistakable. She couldn't see it clearly, but the outline of the creature was enormous, its body coiled like a serpent, its eyes glowing with an eerie light.

The growl grew louder, reverberating through the air, and Evelyn's blood ran cold. Whatever this thing was, it wasn't just an animal. It was something else. Something ancient. Something the forest had called forth.

"We need to move," the man said sharply, his eyes fixed on the creature. "Now."

The woman didn't argue. She pushed Evelyn ahead, her grip firm but steady. "Keep moving," she ordered. "Don't look back."

Evelyn's legs trembled, but she forced herself to run, her heart pounding in her chest as the ground continued to shake beneath her. The firefly's light flickered wildly, barely keeping up with them as they sprinted through the trees.

Behind them, the creature let out a deafening roar, its massive body slithering through the collapsing earth. Evelyn didn't dare look back. The sound alone was enough to terrify her. It was getting closer, its presence looming over them like a dark cloud.

The forest seemed to shift with every step, the trees bending and warping, as if they were alive, reacting to the creature's movements. The path ahead was barely visible, the fog thickening as the night wore on.

"We're not going to outrun it!" Evelyn shouted, her voice barely audible over the chaos.

The man with the bow turned sharply, his eyes meeting hers for a brief moment before he drew an arrow from his quiver. "We don't have to outrun it," he said, his voice calm but determined. "We just have to fight it."

Before Evelyn could protest, the man stopped in his tracks, spinning on his heel to face the creature. His bow was already drawn, the arrow notched and ready.

"What are you doing?" Evelyn shouted, panic rising in her chest.

The woman grabbed Evelyn's arm, pulling her behind a nearby tree for cover. "Let him handle it," she said firmly. "He's fought these things before."

Evelyn's heart pounded in her chest as she peeked around the tree, her eyes wide with fear. The creature was closing in, its massive body coiled like a snake, its glowing eyes fixed on the man with the bow.

The man didn't flinch. He stood his ground, his body steady, his bow aimed directly at the creature's head. The firefly's light flickered behind him, casting long shadows on the ground.

The creature let out another roar, its jaws snapping as it lunged toward him. But the man was faster. He released the arrow with deadly precision, the silver tip gleaming as it flew through the air and struck the creature in its glowing eye.

The creature let out a deafening screech, its body thrashing wildly as it recoiled from the attack. The ground shook beneath their feet, the trees groaning as the creature writhed in pain.

Evelyn watched in disbelief as the man notched another arrow, his movements quick and precise. He didn't hesitate. He aimed for the other eye and released the arrow.

Another screech, another violent thrash. The ground buckled beneath them, the earth splitting in jagged cracks as the creature's body convulsed.

The woman beside Evelyn tensed, her grip on her blade tightening. "It's not dead yet," she muttered.

The creature let out one final roar, its body coiling in on itself as it collapsed into the sinkhole, disappearing into the darkness below. The earth groaned, the ground trembling as the sinkhole sealed itself, the rocks and debris falling back into place.

For a moment, there was silence. The only sound was Evelyn's ragged breathing, her heart pounding in her ears.

The man lowered his bow, his gaze fixed on the spot where the creature had disappeared. His shoulders were tense, his face unreadable.

The woman stepped forward, her eyes scanning the trees. "It's not over," she said quietly. "The forest isn't done with us yet."

Evelyn swallowed hard, her mind racing. The forest had sent another creature after her—something ancient, something powerful. And it wasn't going to stop. Not until it had what it wanted.

"What... what was that thing?" Evelyn asked, her voice trembling.

The man glanced at her, his expression grim. "The forest's guardian," he said simply. "One of many."

Evelyn's blood ran cold. "There are more?"

The woman nodded. "The forest commands more than just beasts," she said. "It bends time and space, warps reality to its will. And it's ancient. My name is Lila," she added, her voice softer. "I've seen this before. My brother and I—this isn't our first fight with the forest."

Evelyn blinked, taken aback by the revelation. "Your brother?" she asked, her voice quiet.

The man turned, his eyes meeting hers. "Tristan," he said. "We've been through this nightmare before."

Evelyn's pulse quickened as she realized the truth. These two weren't just strangers passing through—they had been terrorized by the forest once before. They had survived it. But at what cost?

"The forest took something from us," Lila said quietly, her eyes darkening with the weight of her memories. "It hunted us, tortured us. We lost people—good people—to the forest's curse. We barely escaped."

Tristan's gaze hardened. "But we didn't escape unscathed," he added. "It left its mark on us."

Evelyn swallowed hard, her mind spinning. These two had been through hell, just like her. They knew what the forest was capable of because they had seen it firsthand. And now they were helping her because they knew what was at stake.

Lila's eyes softened as she looked at Evelyn. "We couldn't save them," she said quietly. "But we can help you. The forest has marked you, just like it marked us. And it won't stop until it gets what it wants."

Evelyn's stomach twisted with fear. The forest had sent another creature after her—something ancient, something powerful. And it wasn't going to stop. Not until it had her.

Chapter 5: The Haunted Past

The night had grown darker, the trees seemed to press closer, and the air itself felt thick and suffocating. Every breath Evelyn took tasted damp, as though the forest was trying to fill her lungs with its decay. The ground beneath them shifted unnervingly, as if the earth itself was alive, watching their every step. No matter how far they walked, Evelyn couldn't shake the feeling that they were being followed.

Lila and Tristan moved quickly, but there was an edge to their movements—a restlessness that mirrored the forest's growing aggression. Evelyn could sense it in the way the trees leaned in, their branches gnarled and twisted like skeletal fingers reaching for them. The firefly's light flickered weakly, struggling to keep the darkness at bay.

Finally, they stopped by a large rock formation. The air was thick with tension, and the oppressive silence was broken only by the distant rustling of leaves and the occasional groan of the earth beneath their feet. Even here, there was no safety—just a momentary reprieve from whatever was lurking in the shadows.

Evelyn leaned against the rock, her heart pounding in her chest. She had so many questions, but the suffocating air made it hard to think straight.

"What did the forest take from you?" she asked, her voice barely above a whisper, as though speaking too loudly would awaken something in the trees.

Lila's pacing stopped abruptly. She and Tristan exchanged a look, their eyes filled with an emotion Evelyn couldn't quite place—fear, regret, perhaps both. After a long moment, Lila spoke, her voice hollow, as if the words themselves were painful to recall.

"We thought we could escape," Lila said, her voice trembling. "We thought we could outsmart it."

Evelyn's heart skipped a beat. The forest had already started playing its games with her—twisting reality, sending creatures after her—but what it had done to Lila and Tristan seemed worse.

"It started slow," Tristan added, his voice like gravel, scraping against the heavy air. "A whisper here, a shadow there. At first, we thought it was just the isolation. But the deeper we went into the forest, the more... alive it became."

Evelyn's pulse quickened, her skin crawling as the wind stirred the leaves above them, rustling like a soft, malicious laugh.

"We were here for a camping trip," Lila continued, her voice quiet, almost reverent, as if speaking the memory aloud gave it power. "We were trying to reconnect, just a few nights in the woods. But by the second night, we knew something was wrong."

The ground beneath Evelyn's feet felt as if it was shifting ever so slightly, as though it was breathing—waiting.

Lila's eyes darkened, and she took a deep breath before speaking again. "The forest started playing with us. We'd hear things—whispers in the wind, like voices calling our names. Sometimes, it sounded like people we knew. Friends. Family. Then we'd see things—shadows moving, figures just out of sight."

Evelyn shivered, her heart pounding in her chest. She'd seen the shadows too, felt the whispers crawling through her mind like cold fingers. But the way Lila spoke—it was worse than what Evelyn had experienced so far. Far worse.

"It wasn't just in our heads," Tristan muttered, his eyes distant, haunted. "The creatures came soon after. Not just wolves—things that shouldn't exist. Twisted animals, their bodies warped by the forest. Things that were barely alive but still hunting us."

Lila's hand tightened on the hilt of her blade, her knuckles white. "We fought them off, as best we could. But the forest was always one step ahead, always watching, always waiting for us to slip."

Evelyn's heart raced as a cold gust of wind swept through the trees, carrying with it a low, almost imperceptible whisper. Her skin prickled with fear, the weight of the forest pressing in on her from all sides.

"But it wasn't the creatures that broke us," Lila said, her voice barely audible now. "It was what the forest did to our minds. It twisted everything—made us see things that weren't real, made us doubt ourselves, each other."

Evelyn's breath caught in her throat. She knew what they meant. She had felt the forest's pull—the way it warped reality, twisted her thoughts. But the terror in Lila's voice made it clear that what she had experienced was only the beginning.

"We lost ourselves in there," Lila whispered, her voice shaking. "We couldn't trust anything. We couldn't even trust each other."

Tristan's jaw clenched, his eyes cold and distant. "The forest made sure of that. It made us believe that we were each other's enemies. We started fighting, accusing each other of things that weren't real. The forest used our fears against us, twisted our love into something... dark."

Evelyn's stomach twisted in knots. "But you're still together," she said softly.

Lila's eyes flickered with something dark, something broken. "We didn't come out the same," she said. "Not after what it did to us. Not after what it took from us."

Her voice cracked, and Evelyn's breath caught in her throat as she saw the tears glistening in Lila's eyes. "I was pregnant," she whispered, her voice barely audible. "We didn't know for sure at first, but I started showing soon enough. We were... excited. Happy. But then..."

The wind seemed to howl through the trees, as if mocking their pain. Lila's grip on her blade tightened, her knuckles white. "The forest twisted everything. The stress, the fear—it all became too much. And one night, while we were trying to escape the creatures, I lost the baby."

The air around them grew colder, the forest seeming to close in even tighter, suffocating them with its presence. Evelyn could feel the weight of the tragedy pressing down on them, the loss palpable in the air.

"We barely made it out alive," Tristan muttered, his voice raw with emotion. "But the forest didn't let us go. It still has a hold on us. It took our child, our sanity, and our trust in each other. It twisted everything we were."

Lila's voice was filled with a quiet, simmering rage. "That's why we're here," she said, her voice low and deadly. "I couldn't save my child. But I can make sure the forest doesn't take anyone else."

A sudden rustling in the bushes snapped their attention back to the present. The firefly's light flickered weakly, barely enough to keep the oppressive darkness at bay. The trees groaned as if they were waking, shifting under some unseen force.

"It's coming," Tristan said, his voice tense. His hand moved to his bow, his eyes scanning the shadows.

Evelyn's heart raced, the weight of their story still pressing down on her. But now, she felt something else—a spark of determination. They were right. The forest wasn't going to stop. But she wouldn't let it break her.

Lila drew her blade, her movements swift and sure. "We need to move," she said, her voice steady despite the tension in the air. "Now."

Evelyn nodded, pushing herself off the rock. Her legs trembled, her heart still pounding with fear and grief, but there was no time to think. The forest wasn't done with them yet.

As they began to move, Evelyn cast one last glance over her shoulder. The shadows between the trees seemed darker now, deeper. She could feel the forest watching them, waiting for its next move.

But she wouldn't let it take her. Not like it took Lila's child. Not like it took their sanity.

The worst was yet to reveal itself.

Chapter 6: Secrets in the Scrolls

The forest's ominous silence pressed in around them as they moved through the thick underbrush, the darkness heavy and suffocating. Every step Evelyn took felt labored, her legs trembling with exhaustion and fear. But the memory of Lila and Tristan's story weighed just as heavily on her. What they had been through—what the forest had done to them—was beyond anything she could have imagined.

They had been walking for what felt like hours, with only the faint flicker of the firefly's light guiding them. Evelyn's mind raced, trying to make sense of everything that had happened so far, but the constant pressure of the forest made it hard to think clearly. The whispers had returned, soft and distant, barely noticeable, but they were there, crawling under her skin like a cold breeze.

Lila, who had been walking beside her, suddenly slowed her pace, her eyes catching on something in Evelyn's hands. The firefly's light illuminated the small, tattered scroll that Evelyn had been clutching tightly since they left the clearing.

Lila's eyes narrowed in curiosity. "You've been holding onto that for a while," she said, her voice breaking through the silence. "What is it?"

Evelyn blinked, her grip tightening unconsciously around the scroll. She had almost forgotten she was holding it, the parchment worn from her touch. It had been with her since she first entered the forest, a relic of the past, but one she couldn't quite understand.

"I... I don't know exactly," Evelyn admitted, her voice soft. "It's something I found before all of this started. It feels... important. Like it's connected to the forest somehow."

Tristan, who had been walking ahead, stopped and turned, his gaze sharp. "Let me see it."

Evelyn hesitated for a moment, the weight of the scroll pressing against her palm. She had never shown it to anyone before. But these two—Lila and Tristan—they understood the forest in ways she didn't. If anyone could help her make sense of it, it would be them.

Slowly, she unrolled the scroll, the parchment cracking slightly from age. The firefly's dim light flickered over the words, casting long shadows across the page. The poem, written in delicate, faded script, seemed to shimmer faintly in the darkness.

Lila and Tristan stepped closer, their eyes scanning the ancient text. "What is it?" Lila asked quietly.

Evelyn's throat felt tight as she looked down at the words, the haunting lines that had been etched into her mind since she first found the scroll.

"It's a poem," Evelyn said, her voice barely above a whisper. "I think it's about the forest... or something connected to it."

Tristan's eyes narrowed, his hand resting on the hilt of his bow. "Read it."

Evelyn took a deep breath, the weight of the poem heavy on her chest as she began to read aloud, her voice trembling slightly.

❦

Fireflies of the Heart
In midnight's chill, where shadows creep,
I hear the whispers of hearts asleep.
Through the fog, the fireflies glow,
Flickering lights from long ago.
Ghostly embers, soft and pale,

Their silent dance begins the tale.
A love once bright, now faint, decayed,
Trapped in the dark where memories fade.
Their glow, a breath from distant time,
Flickers in rhythm, a ghostly rhyme.
Each pulse a heart that dared to feel,
Now bound in shadows, cold as steel.
They flutter through the hollow night,
Lost in the veil, beyond the light.
A spark of love that once burned bright,
Now fades to whispers, out of sight.
Beneath the trees, where roots entwine,
The fireflies of the heart align.
Their glow reveals the path we tread,
Through haunted woods where dreams have fled.
In every gleam, a silent cry,
A tear that falls from a forgotten sky.
The night consumes what once was whole,
A flicker lost, a burning soul.
They lead us down a winding road,
Where secrets dwell, and winds erode.
Through ruins old, where echoes ring,
The fireflies weave their ghostly string.
But in the dark, they never die,
These fireflies of the heart still fly.
In every pulse, in every gleam,
They haunt the edges of a dream.
Their light, a mirror of the past,
Reflects the love that couldn't last.
Yet still they dance, yet still they fade,
These haunted lights in night's parade.
So follow them through mist and haze,

Through endless nights and forgotten days.
For in their flicker, faint and far,
Lies the ghostly fire of what we are.

❧

THE SILENCE THAT FOLLOWED was thick, the weight of the poem hanging in the air like a cold mist. Lila's eyes were wide, her face pale as the firefly's light flickered over her features.

Tristan remained silent, his gaze fixed on the scroll, but Evelyn could see the tension in his posture, the way his hand gripped the hilt of his bow just a little tighter.

"What does it mean?" Evelyn asked quietly, her voice trembling.

Lila's throat tightened as she looked at Evelyn, her eyes dark with understanding. "It's a warning," she whispered, her voice barely audible. "The fireflies... they're more than just lights. They're connected to the forest, to the souls trapped here."

Tristan's gaze remained fixed on the poem, his expression unreadable. "The fireflies... they're the hearts of the lost," he said, his voice cold. "The people who never made it out. Their souls, trapped here, forever bound to the forest."

Evelyn's heart pounded in her chest, her mind racing as the meaning of the poem began to sink in. The fireflies—the glowing lights she had followed—weren't just lights. They were the remnants of lost souls, bound to the forest, never able to escape.

Lila's hand trembled as she reached out to touch the scroll, her fingers tracing the faded words. "They're leading us," she said quietly. "But to what?"

The question hung in the air, unanswered. Evelyn's mind raced, fear gnawing at her insides. The fireflies weren't leading them to safety. They were leading them deeper into the forest's grip.

"We need to be careful," Tristan said, his voice tense. "The fireflies... they're not just guiding us. They're watching us."

Evelyn's stomach twisted with fear. The fireflies, the poem—it was all connected to the forest, to the curse that held this place in its grip. And now, it was leading them straight into the heart of the danger.

The shadows around them seemed to deepen, the trees groaning as if they were alive, watching. The forest wasn't done with them yet. And now, more than ever, Evelyn knew that the worst was still to come.

Chapter 7: Into the Depths

The forest pressed in around them like a living, breathing entity. Every step felt heavier, every breath more labored. The fireflies, their eerie glow flickering in the dark, hovered just ahead of the group, leading them deeper into the woods. Their light was faint now, barely illuminating the twisted path that wound its way through the trees.

Lila, her eyes sharp and focused, moved with purpose, her blade drawn and ready. Tristan followed closely, his bow at the ready, his eyes darting between the shadows. Evelyn trailed behind, her heart pounding in her chest. She couldn't shake the feeling that they were walking straight into a trap.

The fireflies pulsed rhythmically, their glow growing fainter with every passing minute. The trees seemed to shift, their twisted branches reaching out like skeletal hands, and the air was thick with the stench of decay. The ground beneath them was soft, almost spongy, as though it had soaked up centuries of death and rot.

"This place... it feels different," Lila muttered, her voice low, almost lost in the oppressive darkness. "We're getting closer to something. I can feel it."

Evelyn shivered, her mind racing with the implications of the poem she had just read. The fireflies weren't leading them to safety. They were leading them deeper into the forest's grip—into the heart of whatever ancient evil lay hidden here.

Tristan slowed his pace, his eyes narrowing as he scanned the path ahead. "The fireflies are growing dimmer," he said, his voice tense. "We need to be careful."

Lila nodded, her grip tightening on her blade. "They're watching us," she said, echoing Tristan's earlier words. "They're guiding us, but not to safety. We need to stay sharp."

Evelyn swallowed hard, her throat dry. "Do you think they're leading us to the heart of the forest?" she asked, her voice barely above a whisper.

Tristan's gaze darkened. "It's possible. Whatever the forest is hiding... it's drawing us in."

The fireflies flickered ahead, their light weak but steady, beckoning them deeper into the woods. The shadows between the trees seemed to pulse, shifting and writhing as though they were alive. Evelyn's pulse quickened, fear gnawing at her insides.

Suddenly, the fireflies darted ahead, moving faster than before, their glow dimming almost to nothing. Lila stopped abruptly, holding up her hand to signal them to halt.

"What are they doing?" Evelyn asked, her voice shaking.

Lila's eyes narrowed as she watched the fireflies' erratic movements. "They're trying to lose us," she said quietly. "They want us to follow... but not too closely."

Tristan drew an arrow from his quiver, his eyes scanning the darkened woods. "It's a game," he muttered. "The forest is toying with us."

Evelyn's heart raced as the fireflies darted further into the darkness, their light nearly extinguished. She could barely see the path ahead now, the trees closing in around them like a suffocating wall. The whispers had returned, louder now, circling in the air around them like a storm of voices, too faint to understand but too loud to ignore.

"We need to keep moving," Lila said, her voice sharp. "Stay close, and don't lose sight of the fireflies."

The group pressed on, their steps quickening as they followed the faint glow ahead. The air grew colder, the wind howling through the trees like a chorus of mournful wails. Evelyn shuddered, her skin prickling with fear. The forest was alive, and it was watching them.

As they moved deeper into the woods, the ground beneath their feet began to change. The soft, spongy earth turned to jagged stone, the path narrowing as the trees closed in on all sides. The air was thick with the scent of moss and decay, and the sound of trickling water echoed through the darkness.

Suddenly, the fireflies stopped, hovering over a dark, gaping hole in the ground. The flickering light cast long shadows across the jagged rocks, revealing a narrow path that led downward into the earth.

Evelyn's breath caught in her throat as she stared at the opening. "What... is that?" she asked, her voice trembling.

Lila and Tristan exchanged a glance, their faces grim. "It's an entrance," Lila said quietly. "To something... below."

The fireflies pulsed once more, their light growing faint as they hovered above the opening, as if urging them to descend into the darkness.

"We're not going down there, are we?" Evelyn asked, her voice tight with fear.

Lila's eyes hardened. "We don't have a choice," she said. "This is where the fireflies were leading us."

Tristan stepped forward, his grip on his bow tightening. "It's a trap," he said, his voice low. "The forest wants us to go down there."

Evelyn's heart raced, her mind screaming for her to turn back, to run, to escape. But there was no escaping the forest. Not now.

Lila took a deep breath, her eyes fixed on the dark entrance. "We go in," she said firmly. "But we stay together. No matter what happens, we don't split up."

Evelyn swallowed hard, her pulse pounding in her ears. She didn't want to go down there. Every instinct screamed that it was a death sentence. But Lila was right. They had come this far, and turning back wasn't an option.

As they prepared to descend into the darkness, the fireflies pulsed one last time before disappearing completely, leaving them alone in the suffocating blackness. The whispers grew louder, more insistent, as though the forest itself was beckoning them forward.

With a final glance at her companions, Evelyn stepped forward, her heart hammering in her chest as they began their descent into the unknown.

The ground beneath them was cold and unforgiving, the jagged rocks sharp underfoot. The darkness was absolute, and without the fireflies' guiding light, the forest felt more hostile than ever. The whispers swirled around them like a storm, louder now, their meaning just out of reach.

As they descended deeper into the earth, Evelyn couldn't shake the feeling that something was watching them, waiting for them. The air grew colder, the shadows closing in, and the sense of dread gnawed at her insides like a parasite.

Suddenly, a low growl echoed through the tunnel, reverberating off the walls. Lila and Tristan froze, their weapons drawn, their eyes scanning the darkness for any sign of movement.

The growl came again, louder this time, and Evelyn felt the hairs on the back of her neck stand on end. Whatever was down here with them—it wasn't friendly.

Lila's voice was barely a whisper. "Stay close. Whatever it is, it knows we're here."

The group moved forward cautiously, their senses on high alert. Every step felt like a risk, every sound a potential threat. The growl grew closer, more distinct, and Evelyn's heart pounded in her chest as she realized that they weren't alone.

A shadow moved In the darkness ahead, and before Evelyn could react, a massive shape lunged at them, its jaws snapping with a feral growl. Lila swung her blade just in time, the metal clashing against the creature's thick hide with a sickening thud.

Tristan fired an arrow, the projectile whistling through the air before embedding itself in the creature's side. But it wasn't enough to stop it. The creature roared in fury, its eyes glowing red in the darkness as it lunged at them again.

Evelyn scrambled back, her heart racing as the creature's massive form loomed over her, its breath hot and rancid. The forest's whispers screamed in her ears, urging her to run, to flee, but there was nowhere to go.

Lila and Tristan fought desperately, their movements swift and practiced, but the creature was relentless. It moved with the forest's unnatural strength, its body twisted and malformed, its hunger for blood insatiable.

As the creature lunged for Evelyn, she closed her eyes, bracing for the impact. But at the last second, Lila's blade found its mark, slicing through the creature's throat with a brutal strike.

The beast let out a final, guttural growl before collapsing to the ground, its body twitching before falling still. The silence that followed was deafening, the weight of the forest's presence pressing down on them.

Evelyn opened her eyes, her breath coming in ragged gasps. The creature lay dead at her feet, its massive form twisted and broken.

Lila wiped the blood from her blade, her face pale but determined. "That was just the beginning," she said, her voice cold. "The forest isn't done with us yet."

Tristan nodded, his eyes hard. "We need to keep moving. Whatever else is down here... it's waiting for us."

As they prepared to move deeper into the earth, Evelyn's heart raced with fear. The forest had led them here, into the belly of the beast, and now they were trapped in its grip.

And she knew, without a doubt, that whatever waited for them in the shadows below was far worse than anything they had faced so far. The air grew colder as they descended further, the oppressive darkness pressing in on them like a weight that was impossible to shake. Even the whispers seemed to take on a more sinister tone, growing louder and more persistent, as though they were taunting them.

Evelyn could feel her legs trembling beneath her as they moved, each step harder than the last. Her mind raced, trying to make sense of everything, but the fear gnawed at her relentlessly. The forest was alive—more than just a force of nature, it was something ancient, something filled with malice and hunger.

Tristan took the lead, his bow drawn, his sharp gaze scanning the ever-tightening tunnel ahead. Lila followed closely behind, her blade at the ready, her eyes constantly flicking toward the walls, as though something might reach out from the very rock and pull them into the abyss.

Evelyn struggled to keep up, her breath shallow, her hands trembling. She couldn't shake the image of the creature they had just fought—its twisted form, its glowing eyes, the way it had come at them with such primal fury. The forest had sent it after them, but for what purpose? To break them? To test their resolve?

A sudden, sharp sound echoed through the tunnel—like claws scraping against stone. Evelyn froze, her heart pounding in her ears as the sound grew louder. It was coming from somewhere deep below, from the very depths of the forest's heart.

"We're not alone," Lila muttered, her voice tight with tension.

Tristan nodded, his gaze never leaving the path ahead. "It's waiting for us."

Evelyn's stomach twisted with fear. She didn't want to know what "it" was.

They continued down the winding tunnel, the air growing colder with every step. The darkness seemed to pulse around them, closing in tighter and tighter, as though the very walls of the forest were alive and breathing. The whispers were louder now, almost deafening, their words incomprehensible but filled with malice.

And then, without warning, the tunnel opened into a vast, cavernous chamber.

Evelyn's breath caught in her throat as she stepped into the space. The chamber was enormous, the ceiling so high it disappeared into the darkness above. The walls were lined with ancient, twisted roots that pulsed with a faint, eerie glow. And in the center of the chamber, a massive stone altar stood, its surface covered in strange, unreadable symbols.

The fireflies had reappeared, their ghostly glow hovering just above the altar, casting long, flickering shadows across the chamber. The air was thick with the scent of earth and decay, and the oppressive weight of the forest's presence was almost unbearable.

Lila and Tristan moved cautiously toward the altar, their eyes scanning the shadows for any sign of movement. Evelyn followed behind, her heart pounding in her chest. There was something wrong about this place—something ancient and evil, something that pulsed with the same dark energy that had twisted the creatures of the forest.

As they approached the altar, the fireflies pulsed once more, their glow intensifying for just a moment before fading again. Evelyn's eyes were drawn to the symbols carved into the stone, their meaning just out of reach, but the sight of them sent a shiver down her spine.

"What is this place?" Evelyn whispered, her voice trembling.

Lila shook her head, her eyes scanning the chamber with growing unease. "It's old," she said quietly. "Older than the forest itself, maybe."

Tristan's jaw tightened as he stared at the altar. "It's not just old. It's a shrine."

Evelyn's blood ran cold at the word. A shrine—to what?

Before she could ask, the ground beneath their feet trembled, a deep rumble that reverberated through the chamber. The whispers grew louder, more frenzied, filling the air with their dissonant chorus. The fireflies darted above them, their light flickering wildly as though they, too, were afraid.

Suddenly, the altar began to glow, the strange symbols carved into the stone pulsing with an eerie, red light. The temperature in the chamber plummeted, and Evelyn's breath came in ragged gasps as the darkness seemed to close in around them.

A low growl echoed through the chamber, so deep and guttural it seemed to come from the very earth itself. The shadows twisted and writhed, and from the far corner of the chamber, a massive shape began to emerge from the darkness.

Evelyn's heart raced as the creature stepped into the faint glow of the fireflies. It was enormous—easily twice the size of the creature they had fought earlier. Its body was twisted and malformed, covered in thick, dark fur that seemed to ripple with unnatural movement. Its eyes glowed with a sinister red light, and its mouth was filled with rows of jagged, razor-sharp teeth.

Lila's grip tightened on her blade, her eyes locked on the creature. "This isn't just a beast," she said, her voice cold. "This is something more."

Tristan raised his bow, his expression grim. "It's the forest's guardian," he said quietly. "And it's not going to let us leave."

The creature let out a deafening roar, its massive form lunging toward them with terrifying speed. Lila and Tristan moved in unison, their weapons ready, but Evelyn's legs refused to move. She was frozen in place, her body locked in fear as the creature's glowing eyes fixed on her.

Lila swung her blade, the metal clashing against the creature's thick hide, but the beast barely flinched. It moved with unnatural strength, its massive claws swiping at them with deadly precision.

Tristan fired an arrow, the projectile embedding itself in the creature's side, but it did little to slow the beast down. The creature roared in fury, its glowing eyes locked on Evelyn as it lunged for her, its claws raised to strike.

Evelyn's mind screamed for her to move, but her body refused to obey. The creature was upon her now, its hot breath washing over her as its claws descended.

At the last second, Lila slammed into Evelyn, knocking her out of the way just as the creature's claws struck the ground where she had been standing.

Evelyn hit the ground hard, the wind knocked out of her. She scrambled to her feet, her heart racing as she watched Lila and Tristan fight desperately against the creature. But it was too strong—too fast. They wouldn't be able to hold it off for long.

The whispers grew louder, more frenzied, as though the forest itself was feeding off their fear. The fireflies pulsed wildly, their light flickering as they darted above the battle.

And then, as if in answer to the forest's call, the ground beneath the altar began to shift. The stone cracked, splitting open to reveal a dark, swirling void beneath. A cold wind rushed through the chamber, carrying with it the scent of rot and decay.

Evelyn's breath hitched as she stared at the swirling void, her mind struggling to comprehend what she was seeing. The void seemed to pulse with dark energy, its presence filling the chamber with an overwhelming sense of dread.

The whispers grew louder still, their dissonant voices merging into a single, haunting chant. The fireflies flickered wildly, their light dimming as the forest's dark power surged through the chamber.

And in that moment, Evelyn realized the terrible truth.

The fireflies hadn't been leading them to safety. They had been leading them here—into the heart of the forest's ancient evil.

The void beneath the altar pulsed, and from its depths, something began to rise.

Chapter 8: The Rising Dark

The chamber trembled as the void beneath the altar pulsed with dark energy, sending waves of cold air rushing through the room. Evelyn's heart pounded in her chest as the force began to rise from the swirling darkness, a shadowy shape that seemed to absorb all the light around it.

The whispers reached a fever pitch, their voices blending into a single, terrifying chant that echoed off the stone walls. The fireflies flickered erratically, their light barely illuminating the chamber as the darkness closed in around them.

Lila and Tristan fought desperately against the creature, their weapons clashing against its thick hide, but the beast seemed unstoppable, its glowing red eyes filled with rage. Every time Tristan fired an arrow, or Lila struck with her blade, the creature barely flinched. It was as though the forest itself was fueling its strength.

Evelyn's mind raced, her body frozen with fear as she stared at the dark shape rising from the void. It was like nothing she had ever seen before—a swirling mass of shadows, its form shifting and contorting as it slowly took shape.

A cold wind howled through the chamber, carrying with it the scent of rot and decay. Evelyn's stomach churned as the whispers grew louder, more insistent, their voices filled with malice.

The creature roared, its claws swiping at Lila with deadly speed. She barely dodged the attack, rolling to the side as the beast's massive claws tore into the stone floor. Tristan fired another arrow, the projectile embedding itself in the creature's neck, but it only seemed to enrage the beast further.

"We can't keep this up!" Lila shouted, her voice strained with exhaustion. "It's too strong!"

Tristan's face was grim as he reloaded his bow, his hands shaking from the intensity of the fight. "We need to find a way out of here!"

Evelyn's eyes darted to the swirling void, the dark shape rising higher and higher. Whatever was coming from that darkness—it was worse than the creature they were fighting. It was something ancient, something filled with malevolent power.

She could feel it in her bones, the cold, gnawing presence that had been lurking just beneath the surface of the forest since the moment she stepped into its depths. The fireflies weren't just leading them into danger—they were leading them to the heart of the forest's curse.

And now, that curse was waking.

The dark shape from the void began to solidify, its form twisting and shifting into something monstrous. Its body was made of shadows, but its eyes—its eyes glowed with the same red light that filled the creature they were fighting. It was like a specter of the forest itself, risen to destroy them.

Evelyn's breath came in shallow gasps as the shape continued to rise, its presence filling the chamber with an overwhelming sense of dread. The whispers intensified, growing louder, more frenzied, until they were all she could hear.

The creature let out anotherr deafening roar, its claws slashing through the air as it lunged for Tristan. He dodged just in time, but the beast's claws caught the edge of his arm, drawing blood. He stumbled back, gritting his teeth as he tried to steady himself.

Lila moved in, her blade flashing in the faint light as she struck the creature's side, but it wasn't enough. The beast roared in fury, its eyes glowing brighter as it swung its massive paw at her, sending her crashing into the stone wall with a sickening thud.

"Lila!" Evelyn screamed, her voice cracking with fear.

Lila groaned, trying to push herself up, but the impact had left her dazed. The creature turned its glowing eyes toward her, its massive form looming over her, ready to strike the final blow.

Without thinking, Evelyn rushed forward, her hands trembling as she grabbed a piece of jagged stone from the ground. She threw it at the creature with all her strength, the rock bouncing off its thick hide. It wasn't much, but it was enough to get its attention.

The beast snarled, Its glowing eyes locking onto Evelyn. Her blood ran cold as the creature turned toward her, its massive body tensing as it prepared to lunge.

But before it could move, a deafening roar echoed through the chamber—a roar that didn't come from the creature.

The dark shape from the void had fully risen now, its form massive and terrifying. Its body was made of pure darkness, but its eyes—they glowed with a sickly red light, burning with malice. It let out another roar, the sound shaking the very foundation of the chamber.

The creature froze, Its eyes darting between the shadowy figure and Evelyn. For a moment, it seemed unsure, as though even it feared what had risen from the void.

The whispers swirled around them, growing louder and more intense, their dissonant voices filled with fear and hatred. The fireflies darted frantically above the altar, their light flickering in the darkness.

And then, without warning, the shadowy figure lunged.

It moved with terrifying speed, its massive form barreling toward the creature. The beast roared in defiance, its claws swiping at the shadow, but it was no match for the dark entity. The shadow engulfed the creature, its form wrapping around the beast like a living nightmare.

The creature let out a final, agonized roar before it was consumed by the shadow, its body disappearing into the swirling mass of darkness.

The chamber fell silent, the whispers suddenly ceasing as the dark figure stood tall in the center of the room, its eyes glowing with malevolent power. The fireflies pulsed weakly, their light almost extinguished.

Lila staggered to her feet, her face pale and her body trembling from the fight. "What... what is that thing?" she gasped, her voice filled with terror.

Tristan gripped his bow tightly, his eyes fixed on the dark figure. "It's the heart of the forest," he said quietly. "The ancient evil we've been trying to stop."

Evelyn's heart raced as she stared at the dark entity. The fireflies had led them here—to this creature, to this ancient force. And now it was free.

The dark figure turned its glowing eyes toward them, its presence filling the chamber with an overwhelming sense of dread. The air grew colder, the shadows deepening as the figure began to move toward them.

"We have to get out of here," Lila whispered, her voice shaking with fear. "Now."

Tristan nodded, his grip tightening on his bow. "We won't survive if we stay."

Evelyn's mind raced as they turned to run, her heart pounding in her chest. The fireflies had led them to this place, but they hadn't led them to safety. They had led them into the heart of the forest's ancient curse—and now, that curse was awake.

As they fled through the darkened tunnel, the shadowy figure let out a deafening roar, its voice filled with hatred and fury. The ground trembled beneath their feet, the very walls of the chamber shaking as the dark entity gave chase.

Evelyn's legs burned with exhaustion, but she pushed herself forward, her fear driving her onward. The whispers had returned, louder now, filling her mind with terror as the forest's ancient evil pursued them.

The fireflies darted ahead, their light flickering weakly as they led the way through the winding tunnel. But Evelyn knew now that they couldn't trust the fireflies. They were leading them deeper into the forest's grip—deeper into the heart of the darkness.

The dark figure's roars echoed through the tunnel, its presence pressing down on them like a weight, suffocating them with fear. Evelyn could feel it getting closer, the cold darkness reaching out for her, trying to drag her down into the void.

They had to find a way out. They had to escape.

But deep down, Evelyn knew the truth.

There was no escaping the forest's curse.

Not anymore.

Chapter 9: The Fractured Path

The tunnel twisted and turned, a dark labyrinth that seemed to shift beneath their feet. Evelyn's heart raced as she sprinted through the oppressive darkness, the air thick with the stench of damp earth and decay. The echoes of the dark figure's roar reverberated behind them, a constant reminder of the ancient evil that had awakened in the depths of the forest.

Lila and Tristan moved ahead, their silhouettes barely visible in the dim light of the flickering fireflies. The creature's growls grew louder, sending chills racing down Evelyn's spine. She fought to keep up, her breath coming in ragged gasps as panic surged within her. They had to find a way out—there had to be an escape from this nightmare.

"Keep moving!" Lila shouted, her voice strained with urgency. "We can't let it catch us!"

Evelyn nodded, pushing herself to run faster, but her mind was racing, too. The memories of the poem lingered in her thoughts, its words echoing ominously. The fireflies were more than just lights—they were lost souls trapped in the forest, and now they were being hunted, too.

As they rounded a corner, the tunnel opened into a wide cavern, the ceiling soaring high above them, lost to the darkness. The walls were slick with moisture, glistening as the faint light of the fireflies danced across the surface. But there was no time to marvel at the eerie beauty; the growl of the dark entity reverberated through the cavern, echoing off the stone walls.

Tristan skidded to a halt, his eyes wide with fear. "We need to split up!" he shouted. "It can't follow all of us!"

"No!" Lila snapped, her voice sharp. "We stick together. If we split up, we'll be picked off one by one!"

Evelyn felt the weight of their decision pressing down on her. The creature was relentless, and every second spent deliberating could cost them their lives. "What if we find a way to trap it?" she suggested, desperation creeping into her voice.

"Trap it?" Tristan repeated, disbelief etched on his face. "How do you propose we do that?"

Evelyn glanced around the cavern, her mind racing. The stone walls were lined with jagged rocks and twisted roots, and in the center stood a large, moss-covered boulder. "If we can lure it here and use the boulder to block its path, we might be able to escape while it's distracted," she proposed, her heart pounding at the thought.

Lila exchanged a glance with Tristan, weighing their options. "It's risky," she said slowly, "but it might be our only chance."

The growl grew louder, and the ground trembled beneath their feet, shaking Evelyn from her thoughts. The creature was closing in, and they didn't have much time.

"Let's do it," Tristan said, determination hardening his features. "We'll lure it to the boulder. If we can block its path, we'll buy ourselves some time."

Evelyn's heart raced as they positioned themselves behind the boulder, its size providing some semblance of cover from the approaching threat. The air crackled with tension as they listened to the growl, now a low rumble echoing through the cavern, reverberating in their bones.

Lila glanced at Evelyn, her expression fierce. "When it comes, we need to be ready. Stay focused, and don't let fear take over."

The growl shifted to a roar, echoing through the chamber like thunder. The darkness seemed to pulse with the creature's rage, and

Evelyn felt the fear tighten in her chest. But she couldn't back down now.

With a deep breath, she stepped out from behind the boulder, calling out to the darkness. "Hey! Over here!" Her voice rang out, shaky but loud enough to pierce through the noise.

The shadows shifted, and the creature lunged forward, its massive form barreling toward her with a terrifying speed. Evelyn's heart raced as she darted back, trying to get to the boulder.

"Now!" Lila shouted.

Evelyn pushed herself forward, rushing toward the boulder. They had to time this right. As the creature lunged for her, she ducked to the side, and Tristan pushed against the boulder with all his might. The stone slid Into place just as the creature's claws reached for her.

The boulder struck the creature, the impact shaking the ground beneath them. It roared in fury, but the boulder held, blocking its path.

"Keep pushing!" Lila yelled, urgency lacing her voice.

Together, they shoved the boulder with all their strength, their hearts racing as they managed to secure it against the entrance of the cavern. The creature snarled, its glowing eyes blazing with anger as it slammed against the stone, but it couldn't break through.

"Let's go!" Tristan shouted, leading the way deeper into the cavern as the creature continued to roar and claw at the boulder.

Evelyn ran behind them, her heart pounding with adrenaline. They had bought themselves some time, but she knew it wouldn't last. The forest was relentless, and the creature would find a way.

As they moved deeper into the cavern, the whispers returned, swirling around them like a storm. The darkness seemed to pulse with energy, and the shadows flickered at the edge of their vision, taunting them.

"What's happening?" Lila shouted over the rising cacophony. "Why are they getting louder?"

Evelyn gritted her teeth, trying to drown out the voices. "I don't know! But we need to keep moving!"

The cavern twisted and turned, leading them down a narrow passage that opened into another chamber. The air was thick with moisture, and the ground was slick beneath their feet. Evelyn glanced around, searching for anything that might offer a clue about their surroundings.

In the center of the chamber stood an ancient stone pedestal, its surface covered in intricate carvings that glowed faintly in the darkness. The whispers swirled around them, rising and falling like a haunting melody.

"Look at that," Tristan said, pointing toward the pedestal. "What do you think it is?"

Lila stepped closer, her brow furrowing as she examined the carvings. "It looks like a ritual site," she said, her voice tinged with unease. "But for what purpose?"

Evelyn felt a shiver run down her spine. She could sense the dark energy emanating from the pedestal, and the whispers grew louder, swirling in her mind with terrifying clarity. It was as if the forest was trying to communicate, to pull them closer to its dark secrets.

But as they approached, the ground trembled again, and the creature's roar echoed through the chamber, sending a jolt of fear through Evelyn's heart.

"We can't keep running forever!" Tristan shouted, his voice filled with desperation. "We need to fight!"

But as they turned to face the creature, the whispers grew louder, more frantic, as though the forest itself was beckoning them forward.

Evelyn's mind screamed for her to turn back, to flee, but she knew there was no escape. The shadows twisted around them, warping their reality, and Evelyn felt a wave of despair wash over her.

And then, from the darkness, the creature lunged again, its jaws wide open, ready to consume them whole.

Evelyn's instincts kicked in. She darted to the side, but just as she did, the creature lunged past her, missing by inches.

In that moment, time seemed to slow. She could see every detail—the way its jagged teeth glistened in the dim light, the fury in its eyes as it pivoted, ready to strike again.

Lila swung her blade, connecting with the creature's flank, but it barely registered her attack. Tristan drew another arrow, determination etched on his face as he aimed for the beast's heart.

Evelyn knew they couldn't keep this up. The creature was too powerful, too fueled by the forest's dark energy. And just as they seemed to have the upper hand, the ground beneath them shook violently.

With a deafening roar, the dark entity from the void surged forward, forcing the creature to turn its attention away from them. The two dark beings collided, the chamber filling with a cacophony of growls and roars, echoing against the walls like thunder.

"Now! This is our chance!" Lila shouted, her voice cutting through the chaos.

Evelyn hesitated for only a moment before following Lila and Tristan. They dashed toward the exit, the whispers rising to a fever pitch around them, filling the air with a sense of dread.

As they fled through the dark tunnel, the chaos behind them intensified. The growls and roars were a terrifying symphony, the sounds of a primal battle echoing in the darkness. But Evelyn couldn't afford to look back; the forest was alive, and she could feel its breath on her neck.

Rounding a corner, they stumbled into a narrow passage, the walls closing in around them. The whispers swirled, taunting and shrieking as they pressed onward, the darkness thickening like a suffocating fog.

"Keep going!" Tristan urged, pushing them forward.

Just as they reached a fork in the tunnel, the ground shook violently, and the shadows around them twisted. The dark entity was behind them, relentless in its pursuit, and Evelyn could feel the malevolent energy surging toward them. The whispers rose to a maddening crescendo, drowning out her thoughts, echoing in her mind like a storm.

"Left!" Lila shouted, her voice cutting through the chaos. Without hesitating, the group veered left, adrenaline pumping through their veins. The passage narrowed even further, the walls closing in like the jaws of a great beast.

Evelyn could feel the walls pulse with a life of their own, as if the forest itself was trying to swallow them whole. She glanced back briefly, catching a glimpse of the creature—a massive, dark form clawing its way through the shadows, its glowing eyes fixed on them with insatiable hunger.

The whispers transformed into desperate pleas, begging her to stop, to turn back, to give in to the darkness. But she couldn't—not now. Not when the weight of Lila and Tristan's lives rested on her shoulders.

"Go faster!" Tristan urged, his voice strained as they sprinted deeper into the tunnel. "It's gaining on us!"

The dim light from the fireflies flickered, casting eerie shadows that danced along the walls. Evelyn felt the air grow colder, her breath coming in ragged gasps. Each step sent jolts of pain through her legs, but she forced herself to push onward, the fear of what lurked behind them driving her forward.

As they rounded another corner, the passage opened up into a vast, dark cavern. The ceiling soared above them, lost to the shadows, and the ground was littered with debris—broken stones, twisted roots, and remnants of what looked like old, ancient rituals. The air was thick with moisture, and the chilling scent of decay hung heavy.

In the center of the cavern stood another altar, similar to the one they had seen before, but this one was adorned with grotesque carvings and symbols that seemed to writhe in the flickering light. The shadows danced around it, and Evelyn felt an overwhelming sense of dread wash over her.

"We can't stop," Lila gasped, scanning the cavern for any signs of escape. "We need to keep moving!"

But just as they were about to turn away, the dark entity emerged from the shadows, its form larger and more intimidating than before. It stood at the entrance to the cavern, blocking their path, its eyes glowing with a sinister red light. The air grew heavy with an unbearable tension, and Evelyn's heart dropped.

"This way!" Tristan shouted, pointing to a narrow tunnel on the far side of the cavern. "We can make it if we hurry!"

With no time to waste, they sprinted toward the tunnel, but the creature moved with terrifying speed, its claws scraping against the stone floor as it lunged for them. The ground shook beneath them, sending tremors through the cavern.

Lila was the first to reach the narrow passage. She squeezed through just in time, the creature's claws just missing her as it crashed into the wall behind her. Evelyn followed closely, feeling the creature's breath hot against her back.

"Go! Go!" Lila shouted, her voice filled with urgency.

Tristan shoved Evelyn forward, the darkness behind them swallowing her whole. The narrow passage twisted and turned, the walls closing in as they raced through. The whispers rose again, frantic and desperate, echoing around them like a chorus of lost souls.

Evelyn's breath came in ragged gasps as they pushed onward, their hearts pounding in unison. The air was heavy, thick with the scent of damp earth and decay, as if the forest itself was trying to suffocate them.

Suddenly, the passage opened into another cavern, this one even larger than the last. The ceiling soared high above them, lost in darkness, and the ground was littered with jagged rocks and debris. In the center of the cavern stood a massive stone altar, adorned with grotesque carvings that seemed to pulse with a life of their own.

"This place feels wrong," Lila said, her voice trembling as she scanned the chamber. "We shouldn't be here."

Evelyn's stomach churned as she took in the sight before them. The altar was covered in bloodstains, and the air was thick with the stench of death. Shadows flickered in the corners of the chamber, and the whispers grew louder, filling her mind with fear.

"We need to find a way out," Tristan said, his voice tense. "This isn't safe."

But as they turned to leave, the shadows coalesced into a dark figure, its glowing eyes fixed on them. The air grew colder, and Evelyn could feel the weight of the creature's gaze bearing down on her.

"Run!" Lila shouted, her voice breaking the spell of fear that held them in place.

They turned and sprinted through the chamber, the creature's growls echoing behind them, getting louder and more menacing with each passing moment. The whispers rose to a deafening crescendo, drowning out their thoughts as they raced deeper into the darkness.

Evelyn could feel the shadows closing in around them, the forest tightening its grip. The path twisted and turned, leading them deeper into the depths of the earth. Each corner they turned felt like a descent into madness, the air growing colder and the darkness thicker.

Just as they reached another narrow passage, the creature lunged forward, its claws raking across the ground as it tried to reach them. Evelyn ducked just in time, feeling the rush of wind as the creature's claws sliced through the air where she had been standing only moments before.

"We can't keep this up!" Tristan yelled, desperation lacing his voice.

"We have to find a way to trap it!" Lila shouted, her eyes wide with fear.

Evelyn's mind raced as they pushed forward. They had to outsmart the forest, to find a way to break free from its grip. But as the shadows shifted and twisted around them, the darkness seemed to whisper their doom.

In the distance, the faint light of the fireflies flickered, guiding them deeper into the labyrinthine tunnels. But with every step, the whispers grew louder, urging them to turn back, to give in to the darkness.

As they ran, Evelyn glanced back at the creature, its glowing eyes locked onto her. It was gaining on them, its massive form looming ever closer. The shadows pulsed with energy, and the air crackled with electricity as the creature's growl echoed in the depths of the tunnel.

"Evelyn!" Lila shouted, her voice filled with urgency. "Keep going! We can't stop now!"

They sprinted forward, their hearts racing as they pushed themselves to the limit. The walls of the tunnel seemed to close in around them, the darkness pressing down like a heavy weight.

Suddenly, the ground beneath their feet shifted, and the passage began to collapse. Rocks tumbled from above, blocking their path and forcing them to turn back.

"Back!" Tristan shouted, his voice cutting through the chaos. "We have to find another way!"

Evelyn's heart raced as they stumbled back into the chamber, the growl of the creature echoing ominously in the darkness. The fireflies flickered weakly, their light dimming as the shadows closed in.

As the creature lunged toward them, Evelyn felt a surge of desperation. They had to find a way out, had to escape the forest's grasp before it was too late.

But the darkness pressed in on all sides, suffocating them with its malevolence. The whispers rose to a fever pitch, filling her mind with terror as the shadows closed in, and Evelyn knew that they were running out of time.

"Stay together!" Lila yelled, her voice strained as she fought to keep the fear at bay. "We'll find a way out!"

But as they turned to flee, the shadows twisted, warping reality itself, and Evelyn realized they were trapped in the forest's cruel game. The darkness was alive, feeding off their fear, and it would not let them go.

With the creature behind them and the whispers echoing in their minds, they sprinted into the unknown, the heart of the forest closing in around them, determined to keep its secrets hidden forever.

Chapter 10: The Storm's Grasp

The trio burst from the depths of the cavern, the cool air hitting their faces like a slap as they stumbled into the open forest once more. The growls and roars of the dark creature faded behind them, swallowed by the shadows of the ancient trees. Evelyn's lungs burned from exertion, but the fear of what lurked behind them drove her forward.

"We did it," Tristan gasped, his breath coming in heavy bursts. "We escaped."

Lila wiped the sweat from her brow, her eyes scanning the darkened woods. "For now," she said, her voice laced with anxiety. "But we're not safe yet. The forest is still hunting us."

Evelyn nodded, her heart still racing. They needed to find shelter—and fast. The sky above was a heavy slate gray, ominous clouds swirling as if the storm was about to break. A chill wind whipped through the trees, biting at their skin.

"Where do we go?" she asked, her voice trembling from exhaustion. "We can't stay out in the open like this."

"There's a thicket not far from here," Tristan said, pointing deeper into the woods. "It should provide some cover, at least until the rain passes."

Without waiting for a response, he led the way, his feet sure as he maneuvered through the underbrush. Lila followed closely, her eyes darting around as though anticipating another attack. Evelyn brought up the rear, her thoughts racing. They had narrowly escaped the creature, but the forest felt alive, its shadows pulsing with a malevolent energy.

The wind picked up, howling through the branches as they reached the thicket. It was dense, filled with thorny brambles and twisted vines, but it offered the shelter they desperately needed. As they pushed through the thick undergrowth, they found a small clearing where the trees formed a natural canopy overhead.

"Here!" Tristan said, motioning for them to gather in the center of the thicket. "This should keep us out of sight for a while."

As they huddled together, the first drops of rain began to fall, softly at first, then increasing to a relentless downpour. The sound of the rain hitting the leaves was deafening, a constant reminder of the storm that had settled around them.

Evelyn pulled her cloak tighter around her shoulders, shivering as the chill seeped into her bones. The cold was relentless, and the rain soaked through her clothing in mere moments. "We need to find food and water," she said, her voice shaking slightly. "We can't just wait here."

"We'll have to go back into the forest," Lila replied, her expression grim. "But we need to be careful. The forest is still dangerous, especially in the dark."

Tristan nodded. "There's bound to be a stream nearby. We can find some berries or roots to eat, too. We just have to be quick."

Evelyn felt a knot of anxiety in her stomach. "What if we run into that creature again? We can't face it without a plan."

"We can't live on fear," Lila said, determination hardening her voice. "If we don't find food and water, we'll be sitting ducks. We need to regain our strength."

As the rain continued to pour, the thicket began to fill with the sound of rushing water, the rhythm soothing yet menacing at the same time. They could hear the distant gurgle of a stream, and Evelyn's mouth watered at the thought of fresh water.

"Okay," she said, steeling herself. "Let's find that stream. But we need to stick together."

Tristan and Lila nodded, their expressions resolute. They couldn't afford to let fear control them any longer.

As they emerged from the thicket, the rain hammered down on them, soaking them to the bone. The forest felt alive, the shadows shifting and pulsing as the storm intensified. The air was thick with moisture, and the smell of wet earth filled Evelyn's nostrils.

They moved cautiously, eyes darting to the trees around them. The whispers seemed to grow louder, a chorus of voices warning them of the dangers that lay ahead. The forest was a maze of shadows, and every rustle of leaves set Evelyn's nerves on edge.

As they crept through the underbrush, the sound of rushing water grew louder, guiding them toward the stream. The path was slick with mud, and Evelyn struggled to keep her footing as they made their way downhill.

Finally, they reached the edge of the stream, its waters flowing swiftly over smooth stones. The sight of it made Evelyn's heart lift momentarily, the cool water sparkling in the dim light.

"Water!" she exclaimed, rushing forward. She knelt by the bank, cupping her hands to drink from the cool, clear flow. It tasted like heaven, washing away the taste of fear and desperation.

Lila joined her, scooping water into her hands. "We should fill our canteens, too," she said, glancing around as if the very forest was watching them.

Tristan stood watch, his bow ready, eyes scanning the trees for any signs of danger. "We need to be quick," he urged, his voice tight. "We don't know how long we'll have before that creature finds us."

Evelyn filled her canteen, the cool water refreshing as it sloshed against her skin. As she rose to her feet, she glanced around the forest, a sense of unease creeping back in. The shadows felt thicker, darker, as if the forest was closing in around them.

"We should look for food while we're here," Lila suggested, wiping water from her face. "Berries or roots would help us regain our strength."

Evelyn nodded, though her stomach twisted at the thought of foraging in the darkened woods. They split up slightly, each searching the area for anything they could eat. The rain continued to pour, creating a constant cacophony of sound, but the dark forest felt unnaturally quiet now.

As they searched, Evelyn couldn't shake the feeling that they were being watched. The shadows between the trees felt alive, watching and waiting. She hurried to pick some wild berries, their tart flavor bursting on her tongue, but every rustle made her jump.

"Over here!" Tristan called from a few paces away. "I found some roots!"

Evelyn quickly moved to his side, but as she reached him, the ground beneath them trembled again. The whispers grew louder, a furious chorus urging them to leave.

"We need to go!" Lila shouted, her voice filled with urgency. "Now!"

Without waiting, the three of them quickly gathered what they could and started back toward the thicket. But as they turned, a low growl rumbled through the trees, freezing them in place.

Evelyn's blood ran cold as she caught sight of a pair of glowing eyes watching them from the shadows, just beyond the reach of the rain-soaked light. The creature was back, and it was not alone.

The shadows shifted, revealing more figures—feral shapes emerging from the darkness, their eyes glowing with the same malevolent light. The forest had unleashed its fury upon them.

"We have to run!" Tristan shouted, drawing an arrow from his quiver.

But as they turned to flee, the shadows lunged forward, and the forest erupted into chaos.

Evelyn felt her heart racing as they sprinted through the thicket, the growls and snarls of the creatures behind them growing louder. The rain pelted down, soaking them to the skin, but the cold was the least of their worries. The forest was alive with danger, and every step felt like a step deeper into a nightmare.

"Stay close!" Lila shouted, her voice barely cutting through the noise of the storm. "We need to find a safe place to regroup!"

Evelyn glanced back, her pulse quickening as she saw the shapes closing in—wild animals with sharp claws and teeth glinting in the weak light. The creature they had just fought was only the beginning; the forest was filled with predators, and they were all hungry.

They pushed through the underbrush, the branches clawing at their clothes, the mud sucking at their feet. Every rustle of leaves sent waves of panic through Evelyn, but she forced herself to keep moving, focusing on the dim outline of Lila and Tristan ahead.

"Over there!" Tristan pointed to a cluster of trees that appeared to form a natural barricade. "We can hide there!"

Evelyn followed as they rushed toward the trees, their hearts pounding with fear. Just as they reached the cover of the thicket, a howl pierced the air, chilling her to the bone. It echoed through the forest, a sound that spoke of hunger and madness, and they all froze.

"What was that?" Lila whispered, her eyes wide with terror.

"Something worse than what we just faced," Tristan replied, his voice grim. "We need to move."

They pressed deeper into the thicket, hearts racing, breath coming in frantic gasps. The rain continued to pour, the ground turning to a slick mire beneath their feet. The shadows grew thicker, darker, and the whispers swirled around them like a tempest, filling the air with dread.

Evelyn felt a cold chill creep down her spine. The forest was a living nightmare, and she could feel its malevolent energy wrapping around her like a serpent, tightening its grip.

AS THEY FOUND A SMALL clearing, they huddled together, panting heavily. The rain drummed on the leaves overhead, creating a cacophony that masked the approaching dangers. Evelyn looked around, her heart pounding as she tried to catch her breath.

"Is everyone okay?" she asked, her voice shaky.

Lila nodded, though her eyes were wide with fear. "We need to figure out a plan," she said, glancing toward the shadows that danced just beyond their view. "That howl... it sounded like a pack."

Tristan's expression darkened as he gripped his bow tightly. "We can't let them surround us. If they do, we won't stand a chance."

Evelyn's stomach twisted with anxiety. She could feel the forest closing in, its dark magic wrapping around them like a shroud. The whispers grew louder, almost mocking her, as if the forest itself reveled in their fear.

"We have to find a way to defend ourselves," Lila said, determination creeping into her voice. "If they come after us, we'll need every advantage we can get."

Evelyn glanced around the clearing, searching for anything that could help them. The ground was littered with rocks and branches, but she knew it wouldn't be enough. They needed something more—something to give them a fighting chance against whatever was lurking in the shadows.

"Over there!" Evelyn pointed to a fallen tree on the edge of the clearing. Its trunk was thick, and its branches extended outward, creating a natural barricade. "We can use that for cover!"

Tristan nodded, rushing toward the tree with Lila at his side. Together, they began to push the trunk into position, creating a barrier between themselves and the darkened woods. The rain continued to pour down, soaking them to the bone, but they worked quickly, adrenaline coursing through their veins.

As they finished fortifying their makeshift shelter, the howl echoed through the forest again, closer this time. Evelyn's heart raced, fear tightening its grip on her. She could feel the eyes of the forest upon them, waiting, watching.

"They're coming," Tristan said, his voice tense as he notched an arrow to his bow. "Get ready."

Evelyn felt a chill run down her spine. "What if they surround us?"

Lila's expression hardened as she glanced at Evelyn. "We fight. We don't let them take us."

The whispers grew louder, swirling around them like a storm, filling the air with dread. The rain dripped from the leaves overhead, creating an eerie rhythm that matched the racing of Evelyn's heart. She could feel the forest pulsing with energy, its malevolent presence bearing down on them.

And then, the shadows shifted.

Emerging from the trees, a pack of feral wolves stepped into the clearing, their eyes glowing like embers in the darkness. They moved with a predator's grace, muscles rippling beneath their matted fur, and their snarls echoed with hunger. The leader of the pack, larger and more imposing than the others, stepped forward, baring its teeth in a menacing display.

"Stay together!" Lila shouted, raising her blade defiantly. "We can't let them split us up!"

Evelyn's heart raced as the wolves encircled them, their growls low and threatening. The creatures' eyes locked onto her, their predatory instincts driving them closer. She felt the primal fear settle in her stomach, but she forced herself to stand tall.

Tristan raised his bow, aiming at the leader of the pack. "One shot—one chance!" he yelled, but the wolves seemed unfazed by his presence, their focus solely on the trio.

Evelyn's mind raced, searching for something—anything—that could help them in this dire moment. She glanced at the fallen tree, realizing they had to use it to their advantage. "We need to create a barrier! Get to the other side of the tree!" she shouted.

With no time to think, they scrambled behind the fallen trunk, their hearts pounding in unison. The wolves hesitated, sensing their movement, their eyes flickering with curiosity and hunger.

"We can use the rocks as weapons," Lila suggested, grabbing a handful of stones from the ground. "If we throw them, maybe it will buy us some time!"

"Good idea," Tristan replied, his eyes never leaving the wolves. "On the count of three, we throw."

Evelyn's breath quickened as she picked up a rock, the weight of it grounding her. "One... two... three!"

They hurled the rocks toward the wolves, the stones flying through the air. The impact startled the pack, causing them to scatter momentarily. The leader let out a furious snarl, its eyes blazing with rage as it turned back toward them.

"Now!" Lila shouted, and they all scrambled back to their feet, ready to fight.

As the wolves regrouped, the dark forest pulsed with energy. The whispers grew louder, as if the very essence of the woods was stirring with excitement, urging the pack forward. The air crackled with tension, thickening with the scent of rain and danger.

The leader lunged, and the pack followed, a blur of fur and teeth. Evelyn barely had time to react, her instincts kicking in as she swung the makeshift weapon she had grabbed—a thick branch—from behind the tree.

"Watch out!" Tristan yelled, firing an arrow into the fray. The projectile struck one of the wolves, sending it tumbling to the ground with a yelp.

But the leader was upon them, its jaws snapping dangerously close to Evelyn. She swung the branch, connecting with the creature's side, and it let out a pained growl, but the force of the impact only seemed to enrage it further.

"Keep moving!" Lila shouted, her voice filled with urgency. "Don't let them surround us!"

Evelyn dodged another attack, adrenaline pumping through her veins as they fought to maintain their ground. The forest was alive with chaos, the shadows twisting and turning around them. The wolves moved with a primal intensity, their instincts driving them to hunt and kill.

Tristan fired another arrow, but the pack was relentless. They were surrounded, the growls and snarls filling the air as the rain poured down, mingling with the sounds of their struggle.

"Get to the stream!" Evelyn shouted, spotting a narrow path that led away from the clearing. "We can use the water to create a barrier!"

Without waiting for a response, she dashed toward the path, Lila and Tristan following close behind. The pack gave chase, their howls echoing in the night as they pursued their prey.

Evelyn's heart raced as they sprinted toward the stream, the sound of rushing water growing louder in her ears. She could feel the wolves gaining on them, their breath hot on her heels.

As they reached the stream, she skidded to a halt, desperately searching for anything that could give them an advantage. The water surged around her ankles, cold and invigorating, but she barely registered it.

"Quick! We can use the water to deter them!" Lila shouted, grabbing a handful of mud from the bank and throwing it toward the approaching wolves.

The mud splattered against the nearest wolf, causing it to yelp in surprise. The leader snarled, hesitating for just a moment, and that was all the time they needed.

"Now!" Tristan yelled, and they grabbed whatever they could find—rocks, mud, branches—and began throwing them at the pack. The water splashed around them, creating a chaotic scene as they fought to drive the wolves back.

The cold rain pelted down, soaking them further, but the adrenaline surged in Evelyn's veins as they stood their ground. The darkness pressed in around them, the forest alive with sounds of battle.

The wolves, caught off guard by the sudden onslaught, began to retreat. Evelyn could see the leader hesitating, its glowing eyes darting between them and the darkness of the woods.

"Push them back!" Lila shouted, her voice fierce. "We can't let them regroup!"

With renewed strength, they pressed forward, throwing everything they had at the wolves. The sound of their growls began to fade as they retreated, disappearing into the shadows from which they had emerged.

As the last of the wolves slipped away, Evelyn felt her heart pounding in her chest. They had survived, but for how long? The whispers still echoed in her mind, and the darkness loomed just beyond the edges of the stream.

Panting heavily, they regrouped, their eyes scanning the forest for any signs of the pack returning.

"What now?" Tristan asked, wiping rain from his brow.

"We need to find a way to communicate with the fireflies," Evelyn said, her voice filled with determination. "They might help us find a safe place."

Lila nodded, her expression serious. "And we need to regroup and plan our next move. The forest won't let us go so easily."

The rain began to lighten, but the tension remained thick in the air. They had escaped the immediate danger, but the forest's ancient curse loomed large. Evelyn's heart raced with fear, but she refused to let it consume her.

As they stood by the stream, the last remnants of the wolves faded into the night, the shadows whispering their secrets. Evelyn knew the fight was far from over. The forest was alive, and it had its eyes on them.

They had to find shelter and recover. The storm was still raging, and they needed a place to rest and regroup. With a deep breath, Evelyn turned to her companions, ready to face whatever came next.

"Let's move," she said, her voice steady. "We need to find a safe place to rest and regroup."

The trio began to move cautiously along the stream's edge, the sound of rushing water blending with the gentle pitter-patter of rain. The air was thick with moisture, and the cool breeze felt refreshing against their skin, but the underlying tension still gripped their hearts.

"Stay alert," Tristan warned, his bow at the ready. "We've only just escaped, and the forest isn't finished with us yet."

Evelyn nodded, her heart pounding in her chest. The weight of the forest felt heavier now, and the shadows loomed larger, twisting in the corners of her vision. Each crack of thunder in the distance sent ripples of unease through her, reminding her that they were not alone.

As they walked, the rain began to ease, but the forest was still drenched, the ground a mire of mud and roots. They picked their way through the slick terrain, eyes scanning for any signs of danger. The shadows felt alive, whispering secrets that sent shivers down Evelyn's spine.

"Look!" Lila pointed toward a clump of trees a short distance ahead. "That looks like it might lead to a cave. We can take shelter there!"

Evelyn felt a flicker of hope as they approached the cluster of trees. The dense undergrowth opened into a small clearing, revealing a dark entrance partially concealed by vines and moss. "Let's check it out," she said, her voice firm despite the flutter of anxiety in her stomach.

They crept closer, their senses heightened. The cave entrance was shrouded in darkness, but Evelyn could see faint signs of an opening, enough for them to slip inside.

"Stay close," she whispered as they stepped into the cool shadows of the cave, the sound of dripping water echoing off the stone walls. The dim light from the fireflies flickered in the distance, illuminating the space with a ghostly glow.

Inside, the cave opened into a larger chamber, the ceiling rising high above them, draped with stalactites that glistened in the dim light. The walls were damp and cool, and the air carried the scent of wet earth and stone.

"This is perfect," Tristan said, relief washing over him as he leaned against the cave wall. "At least we're out of the rain."

Lila dropped to the ground, pulling off her drenched cloak. "We need to catch our breath and figure out our next move."

Evelyn sank down beside her, feeling the adrenaline slowly dissipate. She pulled off her own cloak, wringing it out as best she could. The sound of water dripping echoed around them, a steady rhythm that felt oddly comforting amidst the chaos of the forest outside.

"I can't believe we just faced a pack of wolves," Lila said, shaking her head in disbelief. "I thought we were done for."

"We can't let our guard down yet," Tristan warned, scanning the dark corners of the cave. "If those wolves were after us, the creature won't be far behind. We need to be ready."

Evelyn nodded, her heart still racing as she glanced at the entrance. The shadows loomed large outside, a reminder that danger was still close at hand. But they had survived. For now, they were safe, and that was enough.

"Let's take a moment," she said, trying to steady her breathing. "We need to regain our strength before we decide what to do next."

Lila pulled out a small pouch filled with dried fruit and nuts. "I saved some of these from the last time we foraged. They should help us."

As they shared the food, the tension slowly eased. The warmth of the cave wrapped around them, providing a sanctuary from the storm outside. But even as they ate, the unease lingered at the back of Evelyn's mind. She couldn't shake the feeling that they were being watched, that the forest still had its eyes on them.

"We should discuss our plan," Lila said, breaking the silence. "We need to figure out how to deal with that creature and find a way to communicate with the fireflies."

Evelyn felt a spark of determination as she nodded. "We need to understand the forest's magic. There must be a way to harness it, to use it against the dark forces pursuing us."

"Agreed," Tristan said, his expression serious. "The forest is ancient; it knows things. If we can find a way to connect with it, maybe we can turn the tide in our favor."

But as they spoke, a low rumble echoed in the distance, causing the cave to tremble slightly. The sound grew louder, resonating through the stone walls, and Evelyn felt her stomach drop.

"What was that?" Lila whispered, her eyes wide with fear.

"I don't know," Tristan replied, standing up and peering toward the entrance. "But it doesn't sound good."

The whispers returned, swirling in the air like a tempest, growing more frantic as the sound drew closer. The shadows outside the cave pulsed with energy, and Evelyn's heart raced with dread.

"Get ready!" she warned, her voice barely above a whisper.

Suddenly, the entrance darkened, and the outline of a figure emerged. The shadows warped around it, twisting and writhing as if alive. Evelyn felt a surge of terror wash over her as the figure stepped into the light.

It was a creature unlike any they had faced before—a grotesque amalgamation of shadow and fury, its eyes glowing with a sinister light. The air crackled with dark energy as it advanced, and the whispers reached a deafening pitch, drowning out her thoughts.

"Run!" Lila shouted, breaking the spell of fear that held them captive.

Without thinking, they bolted deeper into the cave, the darkness closing in behind them. The creature's growls echoed through the chamber, the sound resonating with primal rage as it pursued them.

"Don't look back!" Tristan yelled, fear fueling his voice. "We have to find another way out!"

Evelyn led the charge, adrenaline propelling her forward as they navigated through the winding tunnels of the cave. The walls felt as though they were closing in, the darkness threatening to swallow them whole.

The whispers grew louder, swirling around them like a storm. Evelyn could barely hear Lila's voice as she called out, urging them to keep moving, but the terror of the pursuing creature filled her mind.

They stumbled through the darkness, the sound of their footsteps echoing off the walls as they ran. The creature was relentless, its growls echoing in the depths of the cave, promising death with every breath.

"We need to find shelter!" Lila cried, desperation lacing her voice. "We can't keep running forever!"

Evelyn spotted a narrow passage to their right, a glimmer of hope flickering in the shadows. "This way!" she shouted, guiding them toward the opening.

They squeezed through the tight space, the walls pressing against them as they tumbled into another chamber. The air was thick and damp, and Evelyn felt the familiar sense of unease wash over her.

"Where are we?" Tristan asked, panting heavily as they huddled together, their eyes darting around the dimly lit space.

Evelyn scanned the chamber, noticing strange symbols etched into the stone walls, glowing faintly in the darkness. "I don't know, but it feels like we've stumbled into something ancient," she said, a shiver running down her spine.

As the whispers intensified, she felt the weight of the forest's secrets pressing in around them. They had to be careful; every choice could lead them deeper into danger.

"We need to regroup," Lila said, her voice trembling. "We can't let the darkness overwhelm us."

Evelyn nodded, her heart racing. "Let's find a way to understand these symbols. Maybe they can guide us."

They moved cautiously, examining the glowing carvings that adorned the walls. The symbols seemed to pulse with energy, and as they touched one of them, a wave of warmth washed over Evelyn, filling her with a sense of connection to the forest.

"What do you feel?" Tristan asked, his voice a mixture of awe and fear.

"It's... it's like the forest is alive," she murmured, her fingers tracing the intricate designs. "I can sense its history, its pain. It's as if it's calling out to us."

Lila stepped closer, her eyes wide. "What if we can use this connection to communicate? To understand the forest's magic?"

Evelyn's heart raced at the possibility. "We have to try. If we can tap into the forest's energy, maybe we can turn the tide in our favor."

The darkness pulsed around them, the whispers rising to a fever pitch as they focused on the symbols, drawing the energy of the forest into themselves. As they concentrated, the air shimmered, and a low hum filled the chamber, resonating with the rhythm of their hearts.

But just as they began to feel the forest's energy flowing through them, the growls of the creature echoed once more, cutting through their concentration. The shadows outside thickened, and the whispers twisted into screams of panic.

"Quick!" Tristan shouted, his voice filled with urgency. "We need to get out of here before it finds us!"

Evelyn glanced back toward the entrance, dread pooling in her stomach. The creature was closer now, its dark form looming at the edge of the passage.

They scrambled toward the back of the chamber, desperate to find an escape. The symbols glowed brighter as they drew nearer, and Evelyn felt the energy surging around them, pulling them into its embrace.

⚜

WITH A FINAL BURST of determination, Evelyn reached out toward the glowing symbols on the wall, her fingers brushing against the cold stone. A surge of warmth coursed through her, and the whispers shifted, transforming from frantic cries to a soothing melody that seemed to resonate deep within her soul. It was as if the forest was trying to communicate, urging them to listen, to understand.

"Evelyn!" Lila's voice pierced through the fog of energy. "We can't let it catch us! We need to find a way out!"

Evelyn tore her gaze from the symbols, feeling the weight of urgency settle over her. The growls of the creature were now a low rumble, shaking the very ground beneath their feet. "There has to be another exit!" she exclaimed, searching the chamber frantically.

Tristan scanned the walls, his eyes darting from one symbol to another. "Maybe these symbols are a map or a guide! If we can decipher them, they might show us the way out!"

"Let's try!" Lila urged, stepping closer to the wall. She touched one of the symbols, and a pulse of energy shot through her, making her gasp.

"What did you feel?" Evelyn asked, her heart pounding as she joined Lila.

"It's... like the forest is alive," Lila replied, her eyes wide. "It's showing us its history. There's pain here—suffering, but also a promise of protection. If we can channel it..."

"Channel it?" Tristan echoed, glancing nervously at the entrance. "We can't wait! It'll be here any second!"

As if to emphasize his words, the growl intensified, sending chills down Evelyn's spine. She had to make a choice: decipher the symbols and risk losing time, or flee the chamber and face the wrath of the creature that hunted them.

"Maybe the symbols can help us fight back," Evelyn said, her voice firm despite the rising panic. "If the forest can lend us its strength, we might stand a chance."

Lila nodded, her resolve strengthening. "We have to try. Together."

Evelyn closed her eyes, feeling the energy of the forest surrounding her, pulling her in. She focused on the glowing symbols, allowing their warmth to envelop her. A vision sparked in her mind—a path winding through the darkness, leading them toward safety.

"Here!" she exclaimed, pointing toward a series of symbols that depicted a spiral intertwined with vines. "This symbol indicates a safe passage through the thicket! If we follow it, we can find an exit away from the creature!"

"Let's go!" Tristan urged, adrenaline surging through him. The growl of the creature echoed closer, drowning out their resolve.

They rushed to the far side of the chamber, following the path indicated by the symbols. The whispers grew louder, swirling around them like a haunting choir, urging them onward.

As they moved, the chamber darkened, the shadows pressing in tighter. The air crackled with energy, and Evelyn felt the weight of the forest's ancient magic surrounding them, propelling them forward.

"Over there!" Lila pointed to a narrow crack in the wall, just wide enough for them to squeeze through. "That's our way out!"

With no time to waste, they pressed through the opening, the jagged stones scraping against their skin. As they emerged on the other side, the sound of rushing water greeted them, and the storm's fury raged on outside.

Evelyn took a deep breath, the cool air filling her lungs as they found themselves at the edge of a rocky ledge overlooking a dark, swirling river. The water churned violently, the current threatening to sweep them away.

"We can't stay here!" Tristan shouted, peering down at the rushing water. "We have to keep moving!"

But as they turned, the creature's growl reverberated through the darkness, closer than ever. It was relentless, the shadows twisting and contorting around them as if the forest was conspiring against their escape.

"Jump!" Lila yelled, her voice filled with urgency. "We have to make it across!"

Evelyn didn't hesitate. She propelled herself forward, leaping into the air as she landed on the opposite bank, her feet slipping on the wet stones but catching herself just in time.

"Go! Now!" she shouted, urgency lacing her voice as Lila and Tristan followed her lead.

The creature's howl echoed behind them, a spine-chilling sound that fueled their determination. They had to find shelter from the storm, a place to regroup and formulate a plan.

But as they sprinted along the bank, the shadows seemed to close in, thickening with each step. The whispers grew louder, a cacophony of voices warning them of the impending danger.

"Evelyn! Look out!" Tristan shouted, pointing ahead.

Evelyn glanced up just in time to see the trees ahead shift ominously, their branches twisting and reaching out like skeletal fingers. The forest was alive with movement, shadows flickering as if the very trees were coming to life, ready to snatch them into their depths.

"Run!" Lila yelled, her voice piercing the chaos as they sprinted toward a cluster of trees ahead.

The forest roared in response, branches snapping and whipping through the air as the dark entity closed in. The growls reverberated through the air, rising to a fever pitch as they pushed onward, fear propelling them through the chaos.

Evelyn felt the ground tremble beneath her feet as the shadows twisted and turned, the darkness alive with danger. The whispers surged, a torrent of sound that threatened to drown out their thoughts.

As they reached the cluster of trees, Evelyn spotted a narrow gap between the trunks, just big enough for them to slip through. "This way!" she shouted, darting toward the opening.

They squeezed through the gap, tumbling into a small clearing beyond. The trees closed in behind them, blocking the path and providing a momentary reprieve from the pursuing shadows.

Panting heavily, they collapsed against the trunks of the trees, catching their breath. The air was thick with moisture, and the smell of damp earth surrounded them, but they had found a momentary sanctuary.

"What now?" Tristan asked, his voice strained as he leaned against the tree. "We can't keep running like this. The forest is never going to let us go."

Evelyn nodded, the weight of their situation settling heavily on her shoulders. "We need to figure out how to fight back. We can't keep running forever."

Lila looked around, her expression resolute. "Maybe the fireflies can help us. If they're trapped in this forest, they might know a way to escape or even confront the ancient evil."

Evelyn felt a spark of hope ignite within her. "If we can communicate with them, they could lead us to a way out or at least give us some insight into what we're facing."

"But how?" Tristan asked, glancing warily at the shadows beyond the clearing.

Evelyn thought back to the symbols in the cave, the ancient magic that had pulsed through her when she touched them. "If we can find a way to tap Into that energy again, we might be able to reach the fireflies."

Lila nodded, determination filling her eyes. "Then we need to find a place where we can connect with the forest. A spot where its magic is strongest."

Evelyn looked around, her heart racing at the thought. "There's a grove nearby. It's said to be a gathering place for the fireflies, where their magic is most potent."

"Then that's where we go," Tristan said, his voice filled with resolve. "We can't let fear control us any longer."

As the rain began to let up, they prepared to move, gathering their strength for the next leg of their journey. They would confront the forest and the ancient evil lurking within it, drawing on the magic that surrounded them.

But the danger was far from over. The shadows would not easily let them go, and the whispers would continue to haunt them as they ventured deeper into the heart of the forest.

With their hearts pounding in unison, they stepped out of the clearing and back into the dark embrace of the woods, ready to face whatever challenges lay ahead.

Chapter 11: The Gathering Storm

The air hung thick with moisture as Evelyn, Lila, and Tristan made their way deeper into the forest. Each step felt heavy, the shadows swirling around them, whispering secrets that sent chills down Evelyn's spine. The storm clouds above continued to loom, their dark presence a constant reminder of the dangers that lurked within the ancient woods.

"Keep moving," Tristan urged, his voice steady but low. "We need to reach the grove before it gets dark. I can feel the forest's magic intensifying."

Evelyn glanced at Lila, who seemed lost in thought, her eyes scanning the trees as if searching for something just out of reach. "Are you okay?" Evelyn asked, concern lacing her voice.

Lila nodded slowly, but the tension in her posture told another story. "It's just... I can feel it too," she admitted, her voice barely above a whisper. "The forest is restless. It knows we're here."

"Let's focus on the path ahead," Evelyn replied, pushing down her own fear. "We can't let the shadows distract us."

As they pressed on, the atmosphere grew heavier. The rain had finally ceased, but the air felt charged, crackling with energy. Evelyn could sense the forest watching them, waiting for the right moment to strike.

After what felt like an eternity of navigating through twisting roots and thick underbrush, they finally caught sight of the grove—a small clearing surrounded by ancient trees that seemed to hum with magic.

The air shimmered with energy, and tiny glowing fireflies danced within the shadows, their light flickering like ethereal spirits.

"We made it," Tristan breathed, relief flooding his voice.

"Now what?" Lila asked, her gaze fixed on the fireflies. "How do we connect with them?"

Evelyn stepped into the clearing, her heart racing as she watched the fireflies flit about, illuminating the darkness with their soft glow. "I think we need to reach out," she said, recalling the warmth she had felt when touching the symbols in the cave. "We have to show them we mean no harm."

Lila and Tristan followed her lead, forming a circle as they held hands. The air around them thrummed with energy, and Evelyn closed her eyes, focusing on the pulsing light of the fireflies.

"Let the forest guide us," she whispered, feeling the connection grow stronger. "We seek your wisdom and protection."

The fireflies began to swirl around them, their light intensifying as if responding to Evelyn's plea. She felt a warm glow envelop her, a sensation of safety amidst the darkness. The whispers of the forest became clearer, weaving through her mind like a haunting lullaby.

Suddenly, the grove shook with a low rumble, and the ground trembled beneath them. The fireflies flickered in response, their light flickering erratically.

"What's happening?" Lila cried, her grip tightening on Evelyn's hand.

"It's the forest!" Tristan shouted, eyes wide with fear. "It's reacting to our presence!"

The whispers crescendoed into a chaotic roar, and the shadows around the grove deepened, swirling like a storm. Evelyn felt the energy shift, a palpable sense of danger rising as the air grew thick with tension.

"Stay together!" Evelyn shouted, her heart racing. "We need to stay focused!"

But the shadows twisted and contorted, coiling around them like serpents. The fireflies flickered wildly, their glow dimming as the darkness pressed in.

Then, from the depths of the shadows, a figure emerged—tall and shrouded in darkness, its presence suffocating. The air crackled with malevolence as the creature stepped into the grove, its glowing eyes fixated on Evelyn.

"You dare to summon the magic of the forest?" it growled, the voice echoing like thunder. "You have awakened powers beyond your understanding!"

Evelyn felt a surge of terror wash over her as she faced the ancient evil that had haunted her dreams. It was more imposing than she had imagined, its aura dark and twisted, radiating a chilling power.

"We seek your guidance!" she shouted, her voice trembling but resolute. "We only wish to understand the forest's magic!"

The creature laughed, a sound that reverberated through the grove, sending shivers down Evelyn's spine. "You think you can bargain with me? The forest is mine, and I control its magic. You are but pawns In a game far beyond your comprehension."

Lila and Tristan stepped closer, their eyes filled with fear, but also determination. "We won't back down!" Lila shouted, her voice fierce. "We've faced the darkness, and we will not let it consume us!"

The creature's gaze shifted, narrowing on the three of them. "You believe you can withstand the darkness? I will show you what true fear is."

With a wave of its hand, the shadows surged forward, wrapping around Evelyn, Lila, and Tristan like a living thing. The air turned cold, the whispers rising to a fever pitch as they were engulfed in darkness.

Evelyn struggled against the grip of the shadows, fear coursing through her veins. "We have to fight it!" she shouted, desperately trying to hold onto the connection they had forged with the fireflies.

"Focus on the light!" Tristan yelled, his voice cutting through the chaos. "Remember why we're here!"

Summoning every ounce of strength, Evelyn closed her eyes and concentrated on the fireflies' glow, picturing their warmth and safety. She reached out mentally, drawing on the energy of the forest, willing it to protect them.

As the shadows tightened, the fireflies flared brighter, illuminating the darkness with their ethereal light. The whispers shifted from chaos to a harmonious melody, filling Evelyn with strength and resolve.

"Let the light guide us!" she shouted, her voice fierce as she pushed back against the darkness.

The shadows recoiled, the creature's furious growl echoing as the light began to push through. Evelyn felt the warmth envelop her, lifting her spirit as the darkness fought to maintain its grip.

"Together!" Lila shouted, joining Evelyn in channeling their energy into the fireflies. The glow surged, breaking the shadows' hold.

In a blinding flash, the darkness shattered, and the grove erupted in light. The creature howled in rage as it was engulfed, the shadows dissolving like mist in the morning sun.

Evelyn gasped, the warmth of the light washing over her as she stumbled back, breathless. The fireflies swirled around them, illuminating the grove with a soft glow, chasing away the remnants of the darkness.

"What... what just happened?" Tristan panted, his eyes wide with disbelief.

"We fought back," Evelyn said, her voice trembling with adrenaline. "We connected with the magic of the forest. We... we won."

The weight of fear began to lift, replaced by a cautious sense of victory. But as they caught their breath, Evelyn felt a lingering unease. The creature had been powerful, and the darkness would not be easily defeated.

The fireflies danced around them, their glow bright and reassuring. Evelyn knew they had only begun to scratch the surface of the forest's secrets.

"We need to find out what else is lurking in the shadows," Lila said, determination shining in her eyes. "This fight isn't over."

Evelyn nodded, her heart racing. They had faced the darkness and emerged victorious, but she knew the forest was still alive with danger. They had to press on, to uncover the truth hidden within the shadows.

"Let's find that grove," she said, her voice filled with resolve. "We need to tap into the forest's magic again, and we'll do whatever it takes."

With renewed strength, they stepped back into the darkness of the forest, ready to face whatever awaited them in the heart of the woods.

Chapter 12: The Wise One

The trio pushed deeper into the heart of the forest, guided by the faint flicker of fireflies that danced ahead, illuminating their path. Evelyn felt a mix of anxiety and determination; the shadows loomed larger, and every rustle of leaves sent shivers down her spine. The weight of their quest pressed heavily on her, and she couldn't shake the feeling that something significant awaited them in the grove.

As they approached the clearing, the air grew thick with magic, swirling around them like a warm embrace. The fireflies seemed to pulse with life, drawing them closer, their gentle glow beckoning.

"Do you feel that?" Lila asked, pausing to absorb the atmosphere. "It's almost... comforting."

"Or deceptive," Tristan muttered, scanning the treeline for any signs of danger. "We can't let our guard down. The ancient evil is still out there."

They stepped into the grove, the energy around them intensifying. The fireflies swirled in a mesmerizing dance, and for a moment, the chaos of the forest faded away. Evelyn closed her eyes, letting the magic wash over her, feeling a connection to the forest she had never experienced before.

Then, from the shadows at the edge of the clearing, a figure emerged—a tall, lean man with wild white hair and a long beard that cascaded down his chest. His eyes, deep-set and wise, seemed to twinkle with knowledge that spanned centuries.

Evelyn felt a chill run down her spine as he approached, the air crackling with energy. "You've come seeking answers, haven't you?" he said, his voice a low rumble, echoing through the grove like distant thunder.

"Who are you?" Lila asked, her voice a mixture of awe and caution.

"I am Eldrin," he replied, his gaze piercing. "A hermit who has watched over this forest for longer than you can fathom. I've seen its beauty and its darkness."

Evelyn stepped forward, curiosity igniting within her. "We're trying to understand the forest's magic and confront the ancient evil that lurks within it. Can you help us?"

Eldrin regarded her with a knowing smile, his eyes glimmering with ancient wisdom. "The forest is a living entity, filled with secrets and shadows. It remembers all who have walked its paths—both light and dark."

As she met his gaze, Evelyn felt compelled to share her truth. "I returned to the forest because I had no choice," she admitted, her voice trembling slightly. "The nightmares... they were consuming my life. Everything fell apart. I thought I could find answers here."

"What kind of nightmares?" Eldrin asked, his tone shifting to one of genuine concern.

"Visions of darkness, of something terrible lurking just beyond my sight. I felt drawn back here, even when I knew the dangers," Evelyn confessed, her heart heavy with the weight of her admission.

Eldrin nodded, his expression understanding. "The forest calls to those who have lost their way. But you must be careful; it can both heal and harm."

Evelyn instinctively touched the old scrolls clutched in her satchel. Eldrin's eyes narrowed slightly as he observed the movement. "You carry the old scrolls," he stated. "May I see them?"

With a hesitant nod, she pulled out the scrolls, unrolling them to reveal the faded poem and the accompanying symbols. The fireflies seemed to draw nearer, illuminating the parchment with their soft glow.

Eldrin examined the scrolls closely, his fingers tracing the lines of the poem and the symbols. "There is more to these than you realize," he said, looking up at Evelyn. "These contain clues that could lead to escaping the forest forever."

Evelyn's heart raced at the thought. "Escape? You mean there's a way out?"

"Indeed," Eldrin replied, his voice low and filled with gravity. "But the path is fraught with peril. The ancient evil will not allow you to leave easily. It feeds on fear and despair, growing stronger with each soul it ensnares."

Evelyn glanced at her companions, determination flooding her. "We've faced so much already. We can't let it win."

"Your resolve is commendable," Eldrin said, a hint of approval in his eyes. "But you must understand that knowledge without preparation is a dangerous gamble. You will need to gather your strength and trust in the magic of the forest to succeed."

"What do we need to do?" Lila asked, her voice steady despite the weight of the moment.

Eldrin gestured toward the trees surrounding the grove. "To harness the forest's magic, you must connect with the fireflies, as they hold the essence of lost souls. They will guide you, but you must first prove your worthiness."

"What does that mean?" Tristan asked, his brow furrowing.

"It means facing your fears," Eldrin replied, his voice growing stern. "The darkness within you must be confronted. Only then can you unlock the power that resides in these scrolls and within the forest itself."

Evelyn felt a chill run down her spine, but deep within her, a flicker of hope ignited. "What else do we need to find?" she asked, her curiosity piqued.

Eldrin's expression grew serious. "You must search for the other clues hidden throughout the forest. The fireflies can lead you to these hidden locations, but you must be attentive to their movements and heed their guidance."

"The fireflies?" Lila repeated, glancing at the glowing insects circling around them. "How will we know where they want us to go?"

"They will flicker and hover near the clues you seek," Eldrin explained. "But be warned: each location will test your resolve and reveal the darkness that dwells within you. Only by overcoming these trials will you gain the knowledge needed to confront the ancient evil."

Evelyn's heart raced at the prospect. "Then let's find these clues," she said, her voice filled with determination. "We'll face whatever challenges come our way."

"Very well," Eldrin replied, a hint of a smile creeping onto his lips. "Then let us begin the journey to uncover the truth of this forest and reclaim your fate. You will need each other more than ever."

With that, Eldrin began to lead them deeper into the grove, the fireflies illuminating the way as they stepped into the unknown. The whispers of the forest echoed around them, a haunting reminder of the challenges that lay ahead, but with Eldrin's guidance, they felt a renewed sense of purpose.

As they ventured further into the heart of the forest, Evelyn felt the weight of their mission pressing down on her, but she also felt a glimmer of hope. They would confront their fears, discover the forest's secrets, and find a way to escape the ancient evil that sought to consume them all.

Chapter 13: The First Clue

As they followed Eldrin deeper into the grove, the atmosphere shifted ominously. The air hummed with an electric energy, and the fireflies flickered anxiously around them, illuminating the ancient trees that loomed like silent sentinels. Evelyn felt the weight of the forest's history pressing down on her, each step resonating with the echoes of lost souls, whispering secrets of dread and despair.

Eldrin led them to a clearing bathed in the ethereal glow of the fireflies, their light casting eerie shadows that flickered like the remnants of forgotten memories. "This is a sacred place," he announced, his voice low and reverent. "Here, the magic of the forest is strongest. It is where the fireflies gather to share their wisdom."

Evelyn's heart raced with anticipation mingled with trepidation. "What do we do now?"

"The fireflies will guide you to the first clue," Eldrin instructed, gesturing toward the shimmering insects. "But you must be prepared to face the darkness that may arise."

Tristan and Lila exchanged nervous glances, but Evelyn felt a surge of determination. "We can do this," she said, her voice steady, though fear crept into her chest. "We've faced so much already. This is just another challenge."

With that, the trio focused on the fireflies as they began to swirl around them, forming a luminous spiral. The glow intensified, illuminating a path leading deeper into the grove. As the fireflies moved, their light flickered in a rhythmic dance, almost as if they were urging the group to follow.

"Stay close," Eldrin warned, his keen eyes scanning the darkening surroundings. "The forest may test your resolve. Trust in one another."

They moved forward, following the fireflies as they flitted along the path. The shadows deepened around them, wrapping tighter with each step. The air crackled with energy, and Evelyn felt a strange connection growing between her and the glowing creatures. It was as if they understood her fears and hopes, guiding her toward something significant.

As they walked, the temperature dropped dramatically. A bone-chilling breeze swept through the grove, rustling the leaves and sending a shiver down Evelyn's spine. "Did it just get colder?" Lila whispered, her breath visible in the frigid air.

Evelyn nodded, her instincts on high alert. "Something feels off. We need to be careful."

They turned a corner, and the fireflies led them to an ancient oak tree, its massive trunk twisted and gnarled, with roots sprawling across the ground like grasping hands. A sense of foreboding hung in the air, thick and palpable.

"This tree... it feels different," Lila murmured, stepping closer, her voice trembling. "There's something here."

Eldrin approached the tree, examining the markings carved into the bark. "This is no ordinary tree. It has witnessed the passage of time and holds secrets within its core." He reached out and traced the carvings with his fingers, his expression grave. "Look closely; these symbols tell a story."

Evelyn leaned in, studying the intricate designs. They seemed to pulse with energy, mirroring the fireflies' glow. "What does it mean?" she asked, her curiosity piqued, though unease gnawed at her.

Eldrin paused, his eyes narrowing as he deciphered the markings. "It speaks of a past entwined with love and loss—a warning of the ancient evil that seeks to consume those who enter its domain."

As he spoke, the fireflies flickered around the tree, their light dimming in a rhythm that mirrored Evelyn's quickening heartbeat. She felt a connection to the oak, a warmth radiating from its core that enveloped her. It was as if the tree was alive, sharing its history through its presence.

Suddenly, a loud crack echoed through the grove, and Evelyn jumped, her heart racing. "What was that?" she whispered, instinctively glancing over her shoulder.

"Stay focused!" Eldrin urged, turning back to the tree. "The fireflies are guiding you. They want you to discover the first clue."

Evelyn's gaze returned to the symbols. As she concentrated, the fireflies began to swirl more intensely around the base of the tree, illuminating a hollow space where the roots intertwined.

"There!" she exclaimed, pointing to the gap. "There's something there!"

Tristan knelt down, carefully reaching into the hollow. His hand brushed against something smooth and cold. "I think I found it!" he shouted, pulling out a small, ornate box, covered in intricate carvings similar to those on the tree.

Evelyn's breath caught in her throat as they gathered around him, excitement coursing through her. "What's inside?"

Tristan opened the box, revealing a delicate piece of parchment inside, inscribed with flowing script and adorned with tiny drawings of fireflies. "It looks like another poem," he said, reading the first few lines aloud:

"In the heart of darkness, where shadows play,
Whispers of secrets guide the way.
Follow the fireflies, their dance a sign,
In their glow, the lost will align."

As he continued reading, the whispers of the forest grew louder, swirling around them like a tempest. Evelyn felt the pull of the poem's meaning, and the energy in the grove surged. Shadows danced at the edges of her vision, whispering dark promises that sent chills racing down her spine.

"Look!" Lila exclaimed, pointing at the edge of the clearing. The fireflies had formed a glowing path that seemed to beckon them forward. "They want us to follow!"

Eldrin nodded, his expression serious. "This is just the beginning. The fireflies will lead you to more clues, but be prepared. Each location will test your resolve and reveal the darkness that dwells within you. You must be vigilant."

"What do we do if we encounter the ancient evil?" Tristan asked, his voice filled with apprehension, his eyes darting to the shadows creeping closer.

Eldrin's gaze hardened. "You must remember the power of the light. The fireflies are your allies; they will guide you, but you must also trust in yourselves. Fear can be a powerful weapon against the darkness."

With renewed determination, Evelyn nodded. "We won't let fear control us. We'll find the clues and confront the ancient evil."

As they stepped onto the path illuminated by the fireflies, the grove around them began to shimmer with energy. The whispers grew louder, swirling with excitement as they moved deeper into the shadows.

The fireflies flickered In unison, guiding them toward their next destination, a pulse of light leading them further into the unknown. Evelyn could feel the anticipation in the air, mingling with the undercurrent of fear that tugged at her heart.

Each step echoed with the promise of discovery, and Evelyn's spirit soared. She was ready to face whatever lay ahead, armed with the wisdom of Eldrin and the companionship of her allies. They would uncover the forest's secrets, confront the ancient evil, and find a way to escape the darkness that sought to consume them all.

But as they ventured further into the darkness, the forest shifted. The trees seemed to close in, their branches clawing at the air like skeletal fingers. Shadows danced, flickering at the corners of their vision, and the air grew heavy with dread. Every crack of a twig and whisper of the wind felt charged with malice, urging them to turn back.

"Stay together!" Eldrin commanded, his voice cutting through the tension. "The forest is testing us. Trust in the fireflies—they will lead the way."

Evelyn tightened her grip on the box containing the poem, a beacon of hope amidst the encroaching darkness. She took a deep breath, steeling herself against the fear threatening to overwhelm her. They would face this together, and with each clue they uncovered, they would draw closer to the truth and the power that could save them.

After what felt like an eternity of walking, Eldrin finally paused, glancing around. "We should rest," he said, his voice steady despite the darkness that surrounded them. "You need food and drink. There is a small shelter not far from here."

"Thank goodness," Lila said, visibly relieved. "I could use a break."

"Me too," Tristan agreed, rubbing his eyes. "I didn't think the forest could feel this oppressive."

Eldrin led them to a small grove with a gnarled tree providing shelter from the elements. The air felt warmer here, and the whispers softened to a gentle hum. The fireflies danced around them, creating a shimmering barrier of light against the encroaching darkness.

Once settled, Eldrin rummaged through his pack, pulling out a small pouch. "Here, this will sustain you for now." He handed them dried fruit and nuts. "It may not be much, but it will give you the strength you need."

As they ate, Evelyn felt a sense of calm wash over her. The fireflies continued to dance, casting soft light that flickered like stars. But beneath the surface, a current of tension lingered, a reminder of the darkness that threatened to engulf them.

"Eldrin," Evelyn said, her voice steady but edged with curiosity, "what can you tell us about the second scroll? Do you have any idea where it might be?"

Eldrin chewed thoughtfully, glancing toward the fireflies. "The second scroll is said to be hidden within the heart of the forest, guarded by the spirits of those who have lost their way. It holds knowledge of the ancient evil and the key to confronting it. But finding it will not be easy; the spirits are restless and will test your resolve."

"Test our resolve?" Lila echoed, her brows furrowing. "What does that mean?"

"It means you will face illusions, fears, and the shadows of your past," Eldrin explained, his voice grave. "The forest knows what haunts you, and it will use that knowledge against you. To succeed, you must confront these shadows and remain steadfast in your purpose."

Tristan leaned forward, eyes wide. "And if we fail?"

"The consequences could be dire," Eldrin replied, his expression somber. "Many have entered the forest seeking knowledge, but few have returned. The ancient evil thrives on despair; if it senses weakness, it will seize the opportunity to ensnare you."

Evelyn felt a knot tighten in her stomach. "How do we prepare for that? How can we ensure we're strong enough to face whatever is waiting for us?"

Eldrin's gaze softened slightly. "Strength comes from within, but it can also be found in unity. Trust in one another, for you are stronger together. Lean on your allies, face your fears side by side, and do not let the darkness isolate you."

Evelyn looked at Lila and Tristan, seeing the determination in their eyes. "We'll face it together," she affirmed, feeling a surge of courage. "No matter what happens, we won't give in to fear."

"Good," Eldrin said, a hint of pride in his voice. "You must also be vigilant of the fireflies. They will guide you to the second scroll, but they will not reveal its location unless you prove worthy. You must demonstrate your intent to face the darkness and seek the truth."

As they finished their meal, the shadows began to stretch ominously around them, creeping closer like dark tendrils. Evelyn shivered, feeling the weight of the forest pressing in.

"Let's rest for a bit before we continue," she suggested, glancing at the others. "We need our strength for whatever comes next."

"Good idea," Tristan agreed, leaning back against the sturdy trunk of the gnarled tree. "We need to be sharp. Who knows what lies ahead?"

As they settled into a moment of silence, the fireflies continued their gentle dance, providing a sense of comfort amidst the encroaching darkness. But as Evelyn closed her eyes, she couldn't shake the feeling of unease lurking in the shadows.

Suddenly, a loud rustle echoed from the trees beyond the grove, making Evelyn's heart race. The fireflies dimmed, and the air turned cold. "What was that?" Lila whispered, her voice barely above a breath.

Eldrin's expression darkened. "The forest is restless," he warned, his eyes scanning the trees. "It senses our presence and is preparing to test you. Stay alert."

Evelyn's heart pounded as she peered into the darkness beyond their small sanctuary. Shadows moved in the treetops, and the whispers grew louder, swirling with a sinister energy. She gripped the box tightly, feeling the warmth of the poem and the fireflies' glow, but it offered little comfort.

"Evelyn," Lila said softly, breaking the silence, "do you think the fireflies are trying to warn us?"

"They could be," Evelyn replied, uncertainty threading through her voice. "But we need to stay focused. The more we panic, the more the forest will thrive on our fear."

"Do you really believe we can defeat this ancient evil?" Tristan asked, glancing at Eldrin. "What if it's too powerful?"

Eldrin's gaze hardened. "It is powerful, but so are you. You have come this far, and you have the strength to face what lies ahead. Remember, the darkness can be defeated with light—if you believe in yourselves and each other."

The tension in the air thickened, and Evelyn felt the chill creeping up her spine. She took a deep breath, steeling herself for the challenges that lay ahead. "We'll find the second scroll, and we will face this evil. Together."

Just as she spoke, a low growl emanated from the shadows, causing the hairs on the back of her neck to stand on end. The growl was deep and menacing, echoing through the trees and making the very ground tremble beneath them.

"It's here," Eldrin whispered, his eyes narrowing as he turned to face the sound. "Prepare yourselves."

Evelyn felt a surge of fear, her heart racing as she exchanged fearful glances with Lila and Tristan. The air grew thick with tension, and the darkness seemed to pulse with anticipation.

"Whatever happens, we stick together," she said, her voice firm, even as the shadows around them twisted and morphed into threatening shapes.

With that resolve echoing in their hearts, they readied themselves for the encounter, knowing that the forest would test their unity and strength. They would have to confront the darkness not just outside but also within, proving that together, they could withstand the storm that threatened to consume them all.

Chapter 14: Into the Depths

The growl echoed ominously through the grove, a deep, resonant sound that vibrated through the very ground beneath them. Evelyn's heart raced as she turned to Eldrin, who stood tense and alert, his gaze fixed on the darkness where the sound originated. The fireflies swarmed around them, flickering rapidly as if sensing the danger.

"What was that?" Lila whispered, her eyes wide with fear. "What are we up against?"

Eldrin's face was grim as he peered into the shadows. "The forest has awakened. The ancient evil has sensed our presence, and it will not take kindly to our intrusion."

Tristan swallowed hard, his hands clenched into fists. "We can't just stand here! We need to find shelter or something to defend ourselves!"

"We cannot flee," Eldrin replied, his voice steady yet urgent. "If we run, it will hunt us down. We must stand our ground and confront whatever comes our way."

Evelyn felt the weight of the moment pressing down on her. "What do we do?" she asked, desperation creeping into her voice.

"Stay close together," Eldrin instructed. "And remember the power of the light. Trust in the fireflies—they may lead us to a means of protection."

As the growl grew louder, the shadows shifted and danced, forming shapes that appeared to claw at the edges of the grove. The fireflies dimmed, creating an unsettling darkness that wrapped around them like a thick fog.

Then, without warning, a figure burst forth from the trees, a hulking mass of shadow and fury. Its eyes glowed a fierce red, piercing through the dark as it emerged, revealing elongated limbs and a gaping maw lined with sharp teeth.

Evelyn's breath hitched in her throat as fear coursed through her veins. "What is that?!" she gasped, instinctively stepping back.

"Stand your ground!" Eldrin commanded, raising his hands as if to summon the forest's magic. "Trust in the fireflies!"

The creature lunged forward, its growl reverberating in the air, causing the very ground to shake. But just as it reached them, a burst of light emanated from the fireflies, illuminating the grove in a brilliant glow. The shadows momentarily recoiled, revealing the true extent of the creature's grotesque form.

"Now!" Eldrin shouted, urging them to move. "Follow the fireflies! They will show you the way!"

The fireflies darted ahead, their light illuminating a narrow path that wound through the trees. Evelyn's instincts kicked in, and without thinking, she turned to run, Lila and Tristan close behind her.

As they sprinted through the grove, the creature pursued, its growls echoing like thunder in the night. The fireflies led them deeper into the forest, their light flickering desperately as they navigated the twisted roots and underbrush.

"Keep going!" Evelyn urged, her heart pounding as she pushed herself to run faster. "We can't let it catch us!"

The shadows twisted around them, and the trees seemed to close in, forming a labyrinth that threatened to trap them. The growls of the creature echoed behind them, growing closer with each passing moment.

Suddenly, they burst into another clearing, and Evelyn skidded to a halt. In the center stood a massive stone archway, covered in vines and glowing symbols. It radiated an ancient power that pulsed with the same energy she had felt earlier.

"This way!" Eldrin shouted, pointing toward the archway. "It may offer us a chance to escape!"

Without hesitation, they raced toward the archway, the fireflies swirling around them in a protective dance. As they reached the stone structure, Evelyn felt a surge of energy, a warmth that enveloped her like a comforting embrace.

"Get inside!" Tristan yelled, glancing over his shoulder as the creature emerged from the shadows, its red eyes locked onto them.

Evelyn and Lila slipped through the archway just in time, Eldrin following closely behind. As they crossed the threshold, the creature lunged, its claws scraping against the stones, but a barrier of light erupted from the archway, pushing it back with a deafening roar.

Breathless, they stood within the archway, feeling the energy pulsing around them, a barrier that seemed to hold the creature at bay. The air hummed with magic, and the fireflies flickered brightly, swirling in a protective cocoon.

"What is this place?" Lila gasped, her eyes wide as she took in their surroundings. The walls of the archway were covered in more symbols, glowing faintly in the darkness.

"This is a sanctuary," Eldrin explained, his voice steady despite the chaos outside. "A place where the forest's magic is strongest. Here, we can gather our strength and seek answers."

Evelyn took a moment to catch her breath, feeling the adrenaline slowly fade. "But for how long? That creature will be back," she said, glancing back toward the entrance.

"We have time," Eldrin replied, examining the symbols on the walls. "These markings hold the secrets of the forest. We may find guidance here."

As Evelyn looked around, the fireflies began to settle, their glow illuminating the space, revealing intricate carvings of fireflies intertwined with ancient trees and shadows. A sense of calm washed over her, and she felt the weight of their journey lift, if only for a moment.

"Let's examine the symbols," she said, stepping closer to the wall. "Maybe they can tell us how to defeat the creature."

Tristan and Lila joined her, their expressions shifting from fear to determination as they studied the carvings. "If we can decipher these, maybe we can find a way to fight back," Tristan suggested, tracing his fingers over the intricate designs.

Suddenly, a chilling howl echoed from outside the sanctuary, sending shivers down Evelyn's spine. "It's here," she whispered, her heart racing again.

Eldrin's eyes narrowed. "We must act quickly. The ancient evil is relentless."

As they focused on the symbols, the fireflies began to swirl around them, their light pulsating in sync with the energy of the markings. Evelyn could feel a connection forming, a link between the past and their present struggle.

"Let's decipher this," she said, determination igniting within her. "Together."

Chapter 15: The Hermit's Warning

The air inside the archway hummed with ancient energy, and Evelyn could still feel the thrum of magic coursing through the stone walls. But the sanctuary wasn't enough to calm the gnawing unease in her chest. The creature was still out there, lurking just beyond the barrier, its red eyes burning through the night like twin flames. It wasn't finished with them—not yet.

Eldrin knelt beside the symbols etched into the walls, his brow furrowed in concentration. Lila and Tristan stood close by, their eyes flicking nervously between the glowing carvings and the entrance of the sanctuary, where the shadowy figure of the creature lingered in the gloom.

"We don't have much time," Tristan muttered, running a hand through his hair. "That thing will break through eventually."

"We have to decipher these symbols," Eldrin said, his voice low but steady. "There's a reason this sanctuary exists. It holds the key to understanding the forest's power—and the ancient evil we face."

Evelyn stared at the markings, feeling the same strange pull she had felt when she first encountered the scrolls. The symbols seemed to glow brighter when she approached, as if they were calling out to her. Her fingers itched to trace their lines, to understand the story they told.

As she stepped closer, Eldrin glanced up at her. "Do you feel it too?" he asked, his gaze sharp. "The connection?"

Evelyn nodded. "It's like the scrolls... they're tied to this place somehow."

Eldrin's eyes darkened. "Then we're closer to the truth than I thought."

Lila shuddered and wrapped her arms around herself. "I don't care about the truth right now. I just want to get out of here alive."

Eldrin stood and turned toward her, his expression grave. "The truth is the only way out. If we don't understand the forest's magic—if we don't find a way to break the curse—none of us will leave here."

A heavy silence fell over them as Eldrin's words sank in. They all knew he was right. The forest had become more than just a physical place—it was alive, and it was hunting them. The only way to survive was to confront the ancient evil that controlled it.

Evelyn turned her attention back to the symbols. They were more than just markings—they were a language, a code that held the secrets of the forest's magic. But understanding them wouldn't be easy. The fireflies swirled around her head, their light flickering in sync with the pulsing energy of the stones.

"I think... I think I can read some of it," Evelyn said slowly, her fingers brushing against one of the glowing symbols.

Eldrin's eyes widened. "You can?"

She nodded, though uncertainty still gnawed at her. "It's not perfect, but the symbols—they're familiar. Like I've seen them before."

Lila looked at her in confusion. "How is that possible?"

Evelyn hesitated. She had no explanation. Ever since they had entered the forest, she had felt a connection to its magic, an unspoken bond that tied her to the ancient power that lurked beneath the surface. But now, standing in this sanctuary, surrounded by the symbols and the fireflies, the connection was stronger than ever.

"I don't know," Evelyn admitted. "But I can feel it... the magic in this place. It's the same as the scrolls."

Eldrin's gaze was intense. "Then you must try to understand it, Evelyn. The fate of all of us may rest in your hands."

Swallowing hard, Evelyn stepped closer to the wall, her fingers tracing the intricate carvings. As she focused on the symbols, something shifted in her mind. Images began to form, hazy at first, but then clearer—visions of the past, of people who had once walked these same woods. She saw flashes of ancient rituals, of fireflies dancing in the night, and of a great power rising from the depths of the forest, consuming everything in its path.

"The forest..." Evelyn whispered, her voice distant as the visions took hold.

"It wasn't always like this. There was a time when it was peaceful... until the darkness came."

"What kind of darkness?" Tristan asked, stepping closer, his eyes wide with interest.

Evelyn closed her eyes, the images swirling faster now. "An ancient evil... something that was sealed away long ago. But now it's waking up... and it's angry."

Lila shuddered again. "Can we stop it?"

Evelyn opened her eyes and glanced at Eldrin, who watched her with a mixture of awe and apprehension. "We can try," she said softly. "But we'll need more than just the symbols."

Eldrin nodded. "The symbols guide us, but they are only part of the puzzle. We need to find the source of the forest's power—the heart of the darkness. Only then can we destroy it."

Tristan frowned. "And how do we find that?"

Evelyn glanced at the fireflies, which were now darting excitedly around the room, their light pulsing brighter and faster. "The fireflies... they know the way. We just have to trust them."

A low growl echoed from outside the sanctuary, causing all of them to tense. The creature was still there, waiting. But now, with the knowledge they had gained, Evelyn felt a spark of hope.

"We have to move," she said, her voice firm. "We need to find the heart of the forest—before it finds us."

Eldrin nodded, his eyes shining with determination. "Then let's not waste any more time. The fireflies will lead the way."

With a final glance at the symbols on the walls, Evelyn turned and followed the glowing fireflies as they drifted toward the exit of the sanctuary. Lila and Tristan were close behind, their fear replaced by a grim resolve. The creature still waited in the shadows, but now they had a direction, a purpose.

As they stepped through the archway and back into the cold, dark forest, Evelyn could feel the fireflies guiding them, their light cutting through the gloom. The path ahead was dangerous, but it was also the only way to survive.

And somewhere, deep within the heart of the forest, the ancient evil stirred, waiting for them to come closer.

Chapter 16: Whispers of the Forest

The fireflies hovered ahead, their light like delicate lanterns guiding them deeper into the unknown. Every step they took seemed heavier, the weight of the forest's secrets pressing down on them. The air was thick, and the trees seemed to loom closer, their gnarled branches intertwining to form a canopy so dense that it blocked out the sky entirely. The forest was alive, breathing, watching.

Evelyn's heart pounded in her chest as she led the group, her eyes fixed on the fireflies. Their glow was the only thing keeping her grounded in the suffocating darkness. Behind her, Tristan and Lila moved in tense silence, their faces pale but resolute. Eldrin, however, walked with a strange calm, as if he had finally accepted whatever fate awaited them.

"There's something wrong here," Tristan muttered under his breath. "It feels like we're being watched."

"We are," Eldrin said quietly, his gaze scanning the dense undergrowth. "The forest has eyes everywhere. It's been watching us since the moment we entered."

Lila shivered, pulling her cloak tighter around her shoulders. "I don't like this. It's too quiet. I feel like something's about to happen."

Evelyn felt it too—the tension in the air, the way the shadows seemed to stretch and twist as if reaching out to them. The deeper they went, the stronger the sense of being hunted. The ancient evil wasn't far off. It was close, lurking just beyond their sight, waiting for the right moment to strike.

"Stay close to the light," Evelyn whispered, her voice barely audible. "The fireflies will protect us."

But even as she said it, she wasn't sure how much longer the fireflies' protection would last. The forest had grown more oppressive, its malevolent presence thickening with each passing moment. The fireflies flickered uncertainly, their once-steady glow dimming as they ventured further into the depths.

Suddenly, a sharp crack echoed through the forest, like a tree branch snapping in the distance. They all froze, their breath catching in their throats. The sound was too close—far too close.

"What was that?" Lila whispered, her voice trembling.

Eldrin held up a hand for silence, his eyes narrowing as he listened intently. "We're not alone."

Evelyn's heart raced as she scanned the shadows, her hand instinctively tightening around the scrolls tucked into her cloak. The fireflies swirled faster now, their glow flickering like tiny stars about to burn out.

Then, from the darkness, came the faintest of whispers. It was barely audible at first, but as it grew louder, the words became clearer, though they were in a language none of them could understand.

"What is that?" Tristan hissed, his eyes wide with fear.

Evelyn shook her head, her pulse quickening. The whispers seemed to be coming from all around them, weaving through the trees like a sinister melody. And then she realized—they were being lured deeper into the forest, drawn by the voices of the very thing they were trying to avoid.

"Keep moving," Eldrin said, his voice tense. "We can't stop now. The heart of the forest is close—I can feel it."

The fireflies darted ahead again, though their light was faint, their energy waning. They followed the path the fireflies set, though every step felt like a step closer to whatever was hiding in the shadows.

The whispers grew louder, and now they were unmistakable. Evelyn could hear words in the murmurs, dark promises and sinister threats that sent chills down her spine. The fireflies pulsed brighter for a brief moment, casting long shadows that stretched and warped, as if the forest itself was twisting under the weight of the ancient evil.

"We're almost there," Eldrin said, his voice firm but laced with urgency. "We need to hurry."

Evelyn could see it now—a faint glow in the distance, barely visible through the thick trees. It wasn't the light of the fireflies. No, this was something else. Something darker.

"That's it, isn't it?" Lila whispered, her eyes wide with fear. "That's where the heart is."

Evelyn nodded, though a knot of dread tightened in her chest. "Yes. We have to go there."

As they moved toward the eerie glow, the whispers grew deafening, filling their ears with dark, unintelligible words. The fireflies flickered wildly now, their light struggling to stay strong in the presence of such overwhelming darkness.

Suddenly, the ground beneath them shifted. The earth trembled as if something massive was stirring beneath the surface. Lila gasped, stumbling backward as the forest itself seemed to come alive, the roots twisting and writhing like snakes.

"We have to keep going!" Evelyn shouted, pulling Lila back to her feet. "Don't stop!"

But the ground continued to quake, and from the darkness, something massive began to emerge. The trees parted as a monstrous figure, cloaked in shadow, stepped forward. Its eyes burned red, the same as the creature that had hunted them before, but this one was even larger, its form more grotesque.

"It's here!" Tristan shouted, drawing his knife as if it would do any good against the massive beast.

The fireflies surged, their light growing impossibly bright as they swarmed the creature, their glow forming a protective barrier around Evelyn, Lila, Tristan, and Eldrin. The creature roared, its voice like thunder, but it couldn't penetrate the wall of light. Not yet.

"We have to reach the heart," Eldrin said urgently, his eyes locked on the glow ahead. "That's the only way to stop this."

Evelyn's pulse raced as they moved forward, the fireflies guiding their way. The creature roared again, its massive claws striking against the barrier, but the fireflies held strong, their light flickering but never fading.

The glow grew closer, and now Evelyn could see it—a massive stone altar, covered in ancient carvings, pulsating with a dark energy that felt like a heartbeat. The whispers reached a fever pitch, swirling around them like a storm, but they pressed on, the fireflies lighting their path.

"This is it," Eldrin said as they reached the altar. "The heart of the forest."

Evelyn stepped forward, her hand trembling as she reached for the scrolls. The symbols on the altar glowed in response, and she knew—this was what the scrolls had been leading her to all along. The connection between them was undeniable.

But as she placed her hand on the altar, the ground shook violently beneath them. The creature let out a deafening roar, and the fireflies' light flickered dangerously.

"We have to act fast," Eldrin said, his voice strained. "The ancient evil is awakening."

Evelyn closed her eyes, focusing on the energy pulsing through the altar. The scrolls in her hands began to glow, and she felt the power of the forest flowing through her, merging with the ancient magic of the altar.

The whispers grew louder, but Evelyn pushed them aside, focusing on the task at hand. She could feel the darkness rising, but she could also feel the light—the same light that had protected them all this time, the light of the fireflies.

"We can do this," she whispered, her voice steady despite the chaos around them. "We can stop it."

With a final burst of energy, the fireflies surged, their light exploding in a brilliant flash. The creature roared in pain as the light consumed it, its form dissolving into the darkness. The whispers faded, and the ground stilled beneath them.

Evelyn opened her eyes, her breath coming in ragged gasps. The creature was gone. The whispers were silent. And the heart of the forest pulsed faintly, its dark energy weakened but not destroyed.

"It's over," Lila whispered, her voice shaky with relief. "We did it."

Eldrin nodded, though his expression remained grim. "For now."

As they stood in the quiet aftermath, Evelyn couldn't shake the feeling that this was only the beginning. The ancient evil had been weakened, but it wasn't defeated. Not yet.

"We still have work to do," Evelyn said softly, her eyes fixed on the faintly glowing altar. "The darkness is still out there."

And as the fireflies dimmed around them, she knew that their journey was far from over.

Chapter 17: The Shifting Shadows

The silence after the creature's defeat was deafening, as though the entire forest held its breath, waiting. The air remained thick with tension, and Evelyn could feel the weight of their actions settling in. The ancient evil had been weakened, but the dark energy that pulsed through the forest had not vanished. It was merely lurking, waiting for the right moment to strike again.

"We can't stay here," Eldrin said, his voice breaking the heavy silence. He was already scanning the tree line, his face drawn and tired. "The forest won't let us rest for long. We need to keep moving."

"But where to?" Lila asked, her voice shaky. She glanced back at the stone altar, its faint glow barely illuminating the dark woods around them. "We've already found the heart of the forest. What else is there?"

Evelyn felt the scrolls in her hand grow warm again, as though responding to Lila's question. There was more—she could feel it. The forest wasn't done with them. Its secrets ran deeper than they had imagined.

"There's another place," Evelyn said softly, her eyes locked on the faint pulse of the altar. "The scrolls are telling me... there's something else we need to find. Something more powerful."

Eldrin nodded, as if he had been expecting this. "Then we follow the fireflies once again. They've brought us this far—they'll lead us to the next piece of the puzzle."

Tristan sighed heavily, rubbing the back of his neck. "Do we even have the strength for this? The forest is relentless, and I don't know how much longer we can keep running."

"We don't have a choice," Evelyn replied, her tone firm. "If we stop now, the darkness will find us. And it won't let us go."

With a reluctant nod, Tristan fell into step behind her, his knife still gripped tightly in his hand. Lila gave one last, wary glance at the altar before following as well, her hands shaking slightly from the tension of the last few hours.

The fireflies hovered above them, their soft light flickering as if the forest's own energy was draining them. But they pressed forward, deeper into the forest, where the trees grew even more twisted and the air more oppressive.

Evelyn's mind raced as they walked, her thoughts swirling with the images she had seen at the altar. The rituals, the ancient power, the shadowy figure that had been awakened—it was all connected, but the pieces were still scattered, like fragments of a broken mirror. The scrolls held answers, but she still didn't understand the full scope of their power.

After what felt like hours of walking in tense silence, the fireflies began to dim, their light growing fainter with every step.

"They're fading," Lila whispered, her voice trembling. "What does that mean?"

Evelyn didn't respond. She could feel it too—the fireflies were losing their strength, and with them, the light that had protected them from the forest's darkness. The whispers that had haunted them earlier were beginning to creep back in, barely audible but present, like the faint murmur of something waiting just out of sight.

Suddenly, the fireflies surged forward, their light flaring for a brief moment before they darted ahead, disappearing into the thick underbrush.

"Follow them!" Eldrin urged, his voice sharp with urgency. "Quickly!"

They didn't hesitate. With adrenaline spurring them on, they chased after the fireflies, ducking under low-hanging branches and dodging twisted roots that seemed to rise up from the ground, trying to trip them.

The whispers grew louder, more distinct now, but Evelyn pushed them out of her mind, focusing only on the light of the fireflies as they led the way through the forest's tangled maze.

After a few minutes, they burst through the trees and stumbled into another clearing. But this one was different. It wasn't like the peaceful sanctuaries they had found before. This place was wild, chaotic—alive.

The ground was covered in thick, black vines that twisted and writhed as though they had a mind of their own. Above them, the branches of the trees were woven together like a net, casting eerie shadows across the clearing. In the center of the space stood a large, ancient stone structure, much larger and more imposing than the altar they had seen before. It towered above them, its surface covered in the same glowing symbols that had appeared on the scrolls.

But this time, the symbols were different. They were darker, more violent, as though they had been carved into the stone with anger and desperation. The air around the structure pulsed with a sinister energy, thick and oppressive.

"This is it," Eldrin whispered, his voice barely audible. "This is what we've been searching for."

Evelyn's breath caught in her throat as she approached the structure, the scrolls in her hand vibrating with energy. The closer she got, the more the symbols on the stone began to glow, their light pulsing in time with the energy of the forest.

"What is this place?" Tristan asked, his voice hushed.

Eldrin stepped forward, his expression grim. "This is the true heart of the forest. The place where the ancient evil was born."

A chill ran down Evelyn's spine as she stared at the towering structure. She could feel the darkness radiating from it, a malevolent force that had been waiting for centuries to be unleashed.

"The scrolls..." Lila whispered, her eyes wide with fear. "They were leading us here all along, weren't they?"

Evelyn nodded, her hand trembling as she reached for the scrolls. "Yes. And now we have to figure out how to stop it."

The whispers returned, louder than ever now, filling the clearing with their dark, twisted words. Evelyn could feel the weight of the ancient evil pressing down on her, suffocating her with its presence. But she knew there was no turning back. This was the moment they had been preparing for—the moment where they would either defeat the darkness or be consumed by it.

"We have to act quickly," Eldrin said, his voice tight with urgency. "The evil is waking up, and once it fully awakens, there will be no stopping it."

Evelyn took a deep breath, her mind racing. The scrolls had brought them here for a reason. The symbols, the magic, the connection between her and the forest—it was all leading to this moment. She just had to figure out how to unlock the power they needed to stop the ancient evil once and for all.

As she stepped closer to the stone structure, the symbols on the scrolls flared to life, their light burning brighter than ever. The ground beneath her feet trembled, and the air crackled with energy.

"We're running out of time," Tristan said, his voice strained. "Whatever you're going to do, do it now!"

Evelyn nodded, her heart pounding in her chest. She raised the scrolls high above her head, the symbols glowing fiercely in the darkness. The ground shook violently beneath them, and a deafening roar echoed through the clearing as the ancient evil began to stir.

The time had come. It was now or never.

Chapter 18: Awakening of the Ancient Evil

The earth trembled violently beneath their feet, shaking the forest to its core. Evelyn held the glowing scrolls high above her, feeling the ancient magic surge through her body like a torrent. The stone structure before them pulsed with dark energy, each symbol flickering with a life of its own, like it was breathing along with the forest itself.

Tristan, Lila, and Eldrin stood tense and ready, their eyes locked on the stone structure. The fireflies swirled around them in frantic circles, their light dimming as the power of the ancient evil grew stronger.

"We're running out of time," Eldrin said, his voice sharp with urgency. "Whatever you do, Evelyn, you need to do it now!"

The dark whispers that had haunted them since they entered the forest were now deafening, filling the air with menacing words in a language none of them could understand. The shadows in the trees twisted and writhed, reaching out like claws, as though the forest itself had come alive under the influence of the ancient evil.

Evelyn focused, the symbols on the scrolls glowing brighter, illuminating the entire clearing in an otherworldly light. She could feel the power building, the connection between the scrolls and the ancient stone structure becoming clearer with each passing moment.

But something was wrong. The energy from the scrolls was powerful, yes, but it wasn't enough. The ancient evil was too strong, too deeply rooted in the forest. Its presence was overwhelming, and even as Evelyn channeled the power of the scrolls, she could feel the darkness pushing back, fighting to maintain its hold over the land.

"We need more!" Evelyn gasped, her voice strained. "It's not enough! I can't stop it!"

The ground cracked beneath them, and from the fissures in the earth, dark tendrils of shadow erupted, twisting and writhing toward the sky. The ancient evil was awakening, and it was angry.

Tristan stepped forward, his face pale but determined. "There has to be something else! Another way to fight it!"

Eldrin's gaze remained fixed on the stone structure, his expression grim. "There is one way," he said, his voice low. "But it's dangerous—too dangerous."

Lila turned to him, her eyes wide with fear. "What do you mean? What's the other way?"

Eldrin hesitated for a moment, his jaw clenched. "The heart of the forest can only be fully stopped by the same magic that created it—blood magic. A sacrifice."

Evelyn's breath caught in her throat, the weight of Eldrin's words hitting her like a blow. "A sacrifice? You mean one of us has to..."

Eldrin nodded slowly. "Yes. The forest demands balance. The ancient evil was sealed long ago through sacrifice, and now, to stop it, we must do the same."

Lila's eyes filled with tears, her voice trembling. "But... but we can't. There has to be another way."

"There is no other way," Eldrin said, his voice soft but firm. "The scrolls have brought us here for this very reason. The power of the ancient evil can only be bound again by offering something of equal value."

The dark tendrils of shadow moved closer, creeping toward them with every passing second. Evelyn's heart pounded in her chest, the scrolls in her hand growing warmer as the energy surged. She looked at her friends—Lila, Tristan, Eldrin—all of them standing on the brink of something far greater than any of them had anticipated.

"I'll do it," Evelyn whispered, her voice barely audible.

"No!" Tristan stepped forward, his face contorted with anger. "You can't! There has to be another way, Evelyn! We'll find it!"

"There isn't," Evelyn replied, her voice steady now. She had known, deep down, that it would come to this. The scrolls had chosen her, the forest had connected with her, and now she had to see it through. "This is what I was meant to do."

Lila shook her head, tears streaming down her face. "No, Evelyn... please..."

But Evelyn had already made up her mind. She stepped toward the stone structure, the symbols glowing brighter in response to her presence. The whispers grew louder, and the ground shook violently as the ancient evil began to stir.

"Take care of each other," Evelyn said softly, looking back at her friends one last time.

Then, without another word, she raised the scrolls high above her head, channeling every ounce of magic into the stone. The ancient symbols flared to life, casting the clearing in a blinding light. The darkness recoiled, the shadows twisting and thrashing as the power of the forest surged.

The fireflies exploded Into light, their glow merging with the energy of the scrolls. The earth beneath them shook with the force of the magic, and the dark tendrils that had been reaching for them began to dissolve, consumed by the light.

But as the power surged through Evelyn, she felt it—an intense pain, ripping through her body like fire. The magic was too strong, too overwhelming for a human to bear. Her knees buckled, and she collapsed to the ground, the scrolls slipping from her grasp.

"Evelyn!" Tristan cried, rushing to her side as the final burst of energy shot through the clearing.

The stone structure pulsed one last time before going dark, its ancient power sealed once more. The whispers were gone. The forest was still.

But Evelyn lay motionless on the ground, her breath shallow, her body limp from the strain of the magic. She was alive, but barely.

"Evelyn, stay with us," Lila whispered, kneeling beside her, tears streaming down her face. "Please, don't leave us."

Eldrin stood over them, his face solemn. "She's alive, but the magic has taken its toll on her. She's severely injured."

Tristan clenched his fists, his heart pounding with fear and frustration. "We need to get her out of here. Now."

The fireflies, though dimmed, still flickered around them, their light soft and reassuring. The ancient evil had been weakened, but not destroyed. It was still out there, waiting for its chance to rise again.

"Let's get her to safety," Eldrin said, his voice calm but urgent. "We need to regroup. This battle isn't over."

As they carefully lifted Evelyn and carried her away from the stone structure, the forest remained eerily quiet, as though holding its breath. The darkness had been pushed back, but the war was far from won.

Evelyn had survived, but at a great cost.

Chapter 19: Secrets in the Shadows

The fire crackled softly, casting flickering shadows on the walls of the cave where they had taken refuge. The air was heavy with the scent of damp earth, and outside, the forest remained unnervingly quiet. Tristan and Lila sat close to Evelyn, who lay on a makeshift bed of blankets, her body still weak from the overwhelming power she had channeled. Her face was pale, and her breathing slow, but she was alive.

Eldrin, standing just inside the cave's entrance, stared out into the darkness, his expression distant. He hadn't spoken much since they left the heart of the forest, but his presence had remained steady, as though he had been waiting for something—or someone—to break the silence.

It was Evelyn who spoke first, her voice a fragile whisper. "I have to tell you the truth."

Lila turned to her, her eyes filled with concern. "Evelyn, you need to rest. Whatever it is, it can wait."

But Evelyn shook her head, a pained look crossing her face. "No... it can't wait anymore. I've been keeping this secret for too long."

Tristan frowned, exchanging a glance with Lila. "What secret?"

Evelyn's eyes shifted to Eldrin, who remained silent, his gaze still fixed on the darkness outside the cave. Her chest tightened, and she knew that this moment had been inevitable. The forest had forced her to confront the truth she had been running from for so long.

"It's about my ex-lover," Evelyn began, her voice barely audible. "The one I lost... the one I thought I'd never see again."

Tristan's brow furrowed, and Lila's expression softened with sympathy. They had known bits and pieces of Evelyn's past, but she had never spoken openly about the person she had loved and lost.

Evelyn took a deep breath, forcing herself to continue. "He's not just someone from my past. He's the reason we're here... he's part of the darkness that we're fighting."

Lila's hand flew to her mouth in shock, her eyes wide. "What do you mean? How can he be...?"

Evelyn closed her eyes, the weight of her confession pressing down on her. "He's the ancient evil. The creature we've been running from, the darkness that's been hunting us—he's the one behind it all."

Tristan recoiled in disbelief, shaking his head. "That's impossible. How could your lover become... that?"

Eldrin finally turned around, his expression unreadable. "It's true."

The others fell silent, turning to face him. Lila's eyes narrowed with confusion and suspicion. "You knew?"

Eldrin nodded slowly. "I knew from the moment we entered the forest. I recognized the signs, the way the energy of the forest reacted to Evelyn. It wasn't just the ancient evil reaching out—it was him. He's been connected to her all along."

Evelyn's voice broke as she spoke again, her eyes welling with tears. "I didn't know at first. I thought he was gone. But when we got deeper into the forest, I started feeling it—the pull, the memories. He's not the same as he was, but there's still a part of him trapped inside that darkness."

Tristan looked torn between anger and disbelief. "Why didn't you tell us? Why keep this from us when it could have changed everything?"

Evelyn wiped away a tear, guilt gnawing at her. "Because I wasn't sure how to tell you. I thought maybe... maybe I could fix it. Maybe I could save him."

Lila's voice was soft, her hand resting gently on Evelyn's arm. "Do you think he can still be saved?"

Evelyn hesitated, her heart aching at the thought. "I don't know. The darkness has consumed him for so long... but part of me wants to believe that there's still hope."

Eldrin stepped forward, his voice steady and firm. "The darkness may have taken him, but it's not impossible to break its hold. However, you need to understand that freeing him will not be easy. The deeper we go, the more dangerous it becomes."

Tristan's fists clenched at his sides, his expression conflicted. "So what do we do? Keep fighting him, or try to save him?"

Evelyn looked up at Eldrin, her voice quiet but determined. "I can't give up on him. I know the danger, but I have to try."

Eldrin nodded solemnly. "Then we'll help you. But we have to be prepared for the possibility that the man you once knew may no longer exist."

Lila looked between them, her brow furrowed in thought. "If he's part of the darkness, then the ancient evil we're fighting is even more dangerous than we thought. How do we defeat something like that?"

Eldrin's gaze grew distant as he considered their options. "The key to breaking the darkness's hold lies in the forest itself. The scrolls, the magic—they're all connected. If we can find the source of the power that binds him to the evil, we may be able to set him free."

Evelyn felt a flicker of hope ignite in her chest, but it was quickly tempered by fear. The journey ahead was treacherous, and the stakes were higher than ever. The forest had already taken so much from them, and the thought of facing her ex-lover, twisted and consumed by darkness, filled her with dread.

But she couldn't walk away. Not now.

"I'll do whatever it takes," Evelyn said softly, her resolve hardening. "I won't let the darkness take him from me."

Tristan nodded, though the tension in his jaw remained. "We're with you, Evelyn. No matter what."

Lila smiled weakly, offering a reassuring squeeze of Evelyn's hand. "We won't let you face this alone."

Eldrin's gaze was steady, his voice low. "Then we have to move quickly. The forest won't wait, and neither will the darkness. If we're going to save him, we need to act now."

Evelyn nodded, her heart pounding with a mix of fear and determination. The path ahead was uncertain, but with her friends by her side, she knew they stood a chance. The forest had tested them, broken them down, but it had not defeated them.

And as they prepared to set out once more, Evelyn couldn't shake the feeling that this was only the beginning. The ancient evil was stirring, and the battle for her ex-lover's soul had just begun.

Chapter 20: The Path of Shadows

The forest seemed darker now, as if the very air had thickened with the ancient evil's presence. The fireflies, once a reassuring guide, now flickered with uncertainty, their light dimmed by the weight of the shadows. As Evelyn rose from her makeshift bed, leaning on Tristan for support, the reality of the journey ahead settled heavily on all of them. There was no turning back.

Eldrin took the lead, his gaze hard and determined as they left the cave and ventured once more into the depths of the forest. His knowledge of the ancient magic that bound Evelyn's ex-lover to the darkness had become their most crucial tool, but even he knew the path ahead was treacherous.

"We're heading to the heart of the forest," Eldrin said, his voice low but clear. "It's where the binding magic was first done, and where the key to breaking it lies."

Lila, walking close behind Evelyn, looked uneasy. "And what if... what if the forest won't let us reach it?"

"The forest will fight us," Eldrin admitted grimly. "It already is. But if we lose focus, if we lose hope, the darkness will consume us too."

Evelyn gritted her teeth against the pain still coursing through her body. She could feel the ancient magic pulling at her, a faint echo of the power she had tapped into during their last battle. But this time, it was different. It felt colder, more hostile, as though the forest itself resented her for what she had tried to do.

"I can feel him," Evelyn whispered, her voice tight with strain. "He's close."

Tristan's expression darkened. "Is that good or bad?"

Eldrin glanced back at her, his eyes narrowing. "It's a warning. The closer we get to the heart of the forest, the stronger his connection to the darkness will become."

Evelyn shuddered, trying to steady her breath. "He's not himself anymore, but I have to believe there's still a part of him left—something I can reach."

Lila placed a gentle hand on her shoulder. "You've got us. We'll face this together."

As they continued deeper into the forest, the atmosphere grew more oppressive. The trees twisted at odd angles, their branches creating a thick, impenetrable canopy above, and the ground was littered with roots that seemed to pulse with life, like veins of the ancient evil itself. The fireflies, usually so bright and lively, now hovered closer to the ground, their light flickering weakly.

Suddenly, a deep, guttural growl echoed through the trees, freezing them in place. The shadows around them shifted, and from the darkness, something moved—slow, deliberate, and predatory.

"It's him," Evelyn whispered, her heart racing.

Tristan's grip tightened on his knife. "We need to be ready."

Eldrin nodded, his eyes scanning the trees. "Stay close. Don't lose sight of the fireflies."

The growl came again, louder this time, and from the shadows, a figure emerged—tall, cloaked in darkness, with eyes that glowed a deep, unnatural red. It was him—Evelyn's ex-lover. But the man she had once known was barely recognizable now. His form had been twisted by the ancient evil, his body elongated and grotesque, his features sharp and monstrous.

But despite the transformation, Evelyn could still see him—still feel the connection they had shared. Her heart ached at the sight of him, but she forced herself to stand firm, to not give in to the fear.

"Don't come any closer!" Tristan shouted, stepping protectively in front of Evelyn.

The creature stopped, tilting its head as if studying them. Its red eyes flickered, and for a moment, Evelyn thought she saw a glimmer of recognition—a spark of the man he had once been.

"Please," Evelyn whispered, stepping forward despite the pain that shot through her body. "I know you're still in there."

The creature's growl deepened, but it didn't move. The shadows around it seemed to pulse in time with its breathing, like the darkness itself was alive, feeding off his rage and pain.

Eldrin stepped closer to Evelyn, his voice quiet but urgent. "We don't have much time. The longer we wait, the stronger the darkness becomes."

Evelyn nodded, her heart pounding in her chest. "I have to try."

She took a deep breath, her mind racing as she searched for the words that might reach him. "I know you're in there. I know the darkness has taken hold of you, but you're stronger than this. You can fight it."

The creature's eyes flickered again, and for a moment, it took a halting step forward, as though something inside him was struggling to break free. But then the shadows surged, and his body tensed, a snarl escaping his lips.

"Please!" Evelyn's voice broke as she took another step forward. "You don't have to do this! I won't let the darkness take you!"

The fireflies around them began to swirl faster, their light growing brighter as they hovered between Evelyn and the creature. The air crackled with energy, and Evelyn could feel the ancient magic stirring again, but this time, it wasn't the same overwhelming force that had nearly destroyed her. It was gentler, more controlled, as though the forest itself was giving her one last chance.

"I love you," Evelyn whispered, tears welling in her eyes. "I always have. And I know you can hear me."

The creature froze, its red eyes locked on hers. The shadows around it seemed to hesitate, as though they, too, were waiting.

Eldrin watched closely, his hand hovering over the pouch where he kept his magic tools, ready to act if necessary. Tristan and Lila stood on either side of Evelyn, their expressions tense, but hopeful.

For a moment, the clearing was silent, save for the soft buzzing of the fireflies.

Then, slowly, the creature took another step forward. Its eyes flickered again, and this time, the red glow dimmed, replaced by a faint, familiar light—the light of the man Evelyn had once loved.

Evelyn's breath caught in her throat, her heart pounding. "You're still in there," she whispered. "I know you are."

But just as hope surged within her, the darkness roared back to life, the shadows swirling violently around the creature as it let out a deafening snarl. Its red eyes flared bright again, and the ground shook beneath them as the forest responded to its rage.

"No!" Evelyn cried, reaching out desperately. "Don't let it take you!"

The fireflies surged, their light growing brighter, but it wasn't enough to stop the darkness. The creature lunged forward, and Eldrin acted in an instant, raising his hand and summoning a barrier of light between them.

The creature slammed into the barrier, letting out a furious roar, but it couldn't break through.

"We have to move!" Eldrin shouted, his face strained from the effort of holding the barrier. "We can't fight him like this!"

Tristan grabbed Evelyn's arm, pulling her back. "We'll come back. We'll find another way."

Evelyn's heart shattered as she looked into the creature's eyes one last time. "I won't give up on you," she whispered, her voice breaking.

With a final, agonized snarl, the creature disappeared into the shadows, leaving them standing in the clearing, the fireflies' light slowly dimming around them.

Chapter 21: The Fading Light

The silence that followed their retreat was deafening. The forest, once alive with whispers and shadows, now felt hollow, as if it, too, had recoiled from the confrontation. The fireflies, though still present, flickered weakly, their light dimming with every passing moment.

Evelyn's heart was heavy with the weight of what had just happened. Her body trembled, not just from the physical strain but from the emotional toll of seeing her ex-lover consumed by the darkness. The brief flicker of recognition in his eyes had given her hope, but it was fleeting, snuffed out by the overwhelming power of the ancient evil.

"We need to keep moving," Eldrin said quietly, his voice pulling her from her thoughts. His face was drawn, the toll of the battle evident in the lines etched deep in his skin. "The forest will not wait for us to recover. The ancient evil is still growing."

Tristan walked beside Evelyn, his eyes filled with worry. "Are you okay?"

Evelyn nodded, though the gesture felt hollow. "I'll be fine," she whispered, though she wasn't sure she believed it. She had been so close—closer than she had ever imagined. And yet, it wasn't enough.

Lila moved closer, her voice soft and tentative. "You almost reached him, Evelyn. I could see it. He's still in there. We just... we need to find a way to break the darkness's hold on him."

Evelyn forced a weak smile, but the ache in her chest remained. "I know. But it feels like every time I get close, the darkness pulls him back."

Tristan shook his head. "We'll find a way. We won't stop until we do."

Eldrin turned to face them, his expression serious. "There is another place—another source of power we can tap into. But it's dangerous. The deeper we go into the forest, the stronger the ancient evil becomes. The last place we need to go... it's where the darkness was first born."

Evelyn's breath caught in her throat. "Where it was born?"

Eldrin nodded slowly. "The forest was not always like this. It was once a place of light, a sanctuary. But something happened—a rift opened, and the darkness seeped into the heart of the forest. It corrupted everything it touched, Including the people who lived here."

"The people who lived here?" Lila repeated, her eyes wide with surprise.

"Yes," Eldrin said, his voice heavy with the weight of history. "Long ago, there were guardians of this forest, protectors of the magic that flowed through it. But when the darkness came, it twisted them, turning them into what you saw today."

Evelyn's heart sank as she realized the full extent of what Eldrin was saying. Her ex-lover was not the only one who had been consumed by the darkness. He was part of a long line of those who had fallen to its power.

"And you think... if we go to this place, we can stop it?" Tristan asked, his voice filled with doubt.

Eldrin met his gaze, his expression grave. "It's our only hope. If we can reach the source of the darkness, we may be able to sever its connection to those it has taken, including your ex-lover, Evelyn."

Evelyn felt a spark of determination flare within her. She had already come so far, risked so much. If there was even the slightest chance of saving him, she would take it. "Then we go," she said firmly. "I don't care how dangerous it is."

Lila nodded in agreement. "We're with you."

Tristan's jaw tightened, but he didn't hesitate. "We go together."

Eldrin gave a nod of approval. "Very well. But we must move quickly. The forest is shifting, and the longer we wait, the harder it will be to reach the source."

The group pressed forward, their steps careful and deliberate as they ventured deeper into the heart of the forest. The trees grew thicker, their branches twisting and curling into unnatural shapes. The air became colder, and the ground beneath their feet felt more unstable, as though the very earth was rebelling against their presence.

As they walked, Evelyn's mind raced. She had come face to face with the man she once loved, but he had been lost to her. Now, as they journeyed toward the source of the ancient evil, she couldn't shake the feeling that their next encounter would be even more perilous. The darkness had taken him once—could she truly bring him back?

Hours passed as they continued through the thickening forest, the fireflies guiding them through the labyrinth of trees and shadow. Each step felt heavier than the last, the oppressive energy of the forest bearing down on them.

Finally, they reached the edge of a vast clearing. At its center stood a towering, twisted tree, its bark blackened and scarred, its branches gnarled and reaching toward the sky like skeletal arms. The ground around it was barren, devoid of life, and the air hummed with a malevolent energy that made Evelyn's skin crawl.

"This is it," Eldrin said, his voice barely above a whisper. "The place where the darkness was born."

Evelyn stared at the tree, her heart pounding in her chest. This was where it had all begun—the source of the ancient evil that had corrupted the forest, and the only place where they might find the power to stop it.

Lila's voice wavered as she spoke. "What do we do now?"

Eldrin stepped forward, his eyes fixed on the twisted tree. "We confront it. The darkness will not let us pass without a fight."

Tristan clenched his fists, readying himself for whatever came next. "Then let's finish this."

Evelyn swallowed hard, her gaze locked on the tree. She could feel the darkness pulsing from it, a deep, ancient power that seemed to resonate with the very core of her being. This was where her journey had led her, where she would face the ultimate test.

As they approached the tree, the shadows around them shifted, and the air grew colder. The fireflies flickered erratically, their light struggling to pierce the gloom. And then, from the darkness, a figure emerged.

It was him—her ex-lover. The man she had once known, now twisted and consumed by the ancient evil. His eyes glowed with a fierce red light, and the shadows around him writhed like living creatures.

"Evelyn," he whispered, his voice echoing through the clearing. "You shouldn't have come."

Evelyn's heart ached at the sound of his voice, but she stood her ground. "I'm not leaving without you."

The man's lips twisted into a cruel smile, his eyes flashing with a mix of sorrow and malice. "There's nothing left of me to save."

Eldrin stepped forward, his voice steady. "We're going to break the darkness's hold on you. We're going to free you."

The man laughed, the sound hollow and broken. "You can't free me. I am the darkness now."

Evelyn's resolve wavered for a moment, but she forced herself to speak. "I won't believe that. I know you're still in there, and I'm not giving up on you."

The shadows around him swirled violently, and the air crackled with dark energy. "You've already lost," he snarled, his voice deepening. "The darkness will consume you, just as it consumed me."

The fireflies surged, their light flaring as if in response to his words. Eldrin raised his hand, summoning the protective barrier of light they had used before.

"We're not giving up," Eldrin said, his voice strong. "Not on you, and not on this forest."

The man's eyes flared with rage, and the shadows exploded outward, rushing toward them with terrifying speed. Evelyn braced herself, her heart pounding as the darkness closed in.

The final battle had begun.

Chapter 22: Battle for the Soul

The air cracked with energy as the shadows surged toward them, swirling like a storm of darkness that threatened to swallow everything in its path. Evelyn's heart raced, but she held her ground, her gaze fixed on the twisted figure of her ex-lover, now consumed by the ancient evil. The fireflies darted frantically around her, their light flickering as they struggled against the overwhelming force of the shadows.

"Get ready!" Eldrin shouted, raising his hand to strengthen the barrier of light that surrounded them. The magic pulsed, pushing back the advancing darkness, but Evelyn could feel the strain in Eldrin's voice. The ancient evil was too strong, too deeply rooted in the forest.

Tristan and Lila stood on either side of Evelyn, their faces pale but determined. Tristan had his knife drawn, though he knew it would do little good against the forces they faced. Lila's hands trembled, but she kept close to Evelyn, ready to protect her friend no matter the cost.

"We can't let the darkness take us," Tristan muttered through clenched teeth. "We need to break through."

Eldrin's voice was tense. "I can hold the barrier, but it won't last forever. Evelyn, you have to reach him."

Evelyn's eyes locked on her ex-lover. He stood just beyond the barrier, the shadows twisting around him like living creatures, his red eyes burning with fury and sorrow. His voice echoed through the clearing, cold and distant. "You're wasting your time. There's no saving me."

Evelyn swallowed hard, pushing down the fear that threatened to overwhelm her. "I don't believe that. I know you're still in there. I know the man I loved isn't gone."

The figure stepped closer, his smile cruel. "The man you loved is dead. I am the darkness now."

For a brief moment, the shadows parted, and Evelyn saw a flicker of something in his eyes—something human, something familiar. It was only for an instant, but it was enough. She knew he was still in there, buried beneath the darkness, but fighting to break free.

"We have to weaken the darkness," Eldrin said urgently. "If we can break its hold, even for a moment, we can reach him."

"How?" Lila asked, her voice tight with fear. "How do we fight something like this?"

"The fireflies," Evelyn said suddenly, her voice filled with a sudden clarity. "They're the key. They've been protecting us this whole time. They know the magic of the forest."

Eldrin nodded, his eyes narrowing in concentration. "Yes, the fireflies are part of the forest's light. If we can channel their energy, we might be able to drive the darkness back long enough to reach him."

The fireflies swirled around them, their light flickering in time with the pulsing darkness. Evelyn could feel their energy, the gentle hum of their magic, and she knew that they were more than just guides—they were guardians, protectors of the forest's ancient power.

"We need to focus," Eldrin said, his voice firm. "Everyone, concentrate on the fireflies. Let their light strengthen the barrier."

Tristan and Lila exchanged nervous glances but did as Eldrin instructed, their eyes fixed on the fireflies as they darted through the air. Evelyn closed her eyes, focusing on the light, feeling the warmth of their magic wash over her.

As they concentrated, the fireflies' glow intensified, their light growing brighter and stronger. The barrier around them pulsed with renewed energy, pushing the shadows back inch by inch. The air crackled with power, and for the first time, Evelyn felt a spark of hope.

The darkness recoiled, and her ex-lover's form flickered, the shadows around him wavering. His red eyes dimmed, just for a moment, and Evelyn knew it was time.

"Now!" Eldrin shouted, his voice filled with urgency. "Evelyn, reach him now!"

Evelyn stepped forward, her heart pounding in her chest. The barrier flickered but held strong, the fireflies swirling around her like a protective halo. She moved closer to the man she had once loved, her voice soft but filled with determination.

"I know you're still in there," she whispered, her eyes searching his. "I know you can hear me. You're not the darkness—you're stronger than it. Fight it. Come back to me."

For a moment, he hesitated, his body tensing as though he was struggling against an unseen force. The shadows writhed around him, but the fireflies' light held them at bay. His red eyes flickered again, and Evelyn saw something she hadn't seen in a long time—recognition.

"You don't have to be this," Evelyn continued, her voice breaking with emotion. "You don't have to let the darkness take you. I'm here, and I'm not giving up on you."

The air around them seemed to still, the shadows pausing in their relentless assault. For a brief, fleeting moment, the man stepped forward, his hand reaching out to hers. His red eyes softened, and the twisted features of his face seemed to relax.

"Evelyn..." he whispered, his voice raw and broken.

Hope surged in Evelyn's chest, and she reached for his hand, her fingers brushing against his. "I'm here," she said, her voice trembling with emotion. "I've always been here."

But just as their hands touched, the shadows roared back to life, surging with renewed fury. The fireflies' light faltered, and the darkness swirled violently around them, pulling him back. He let out a pained cry as the shadows consumed him once more, his eyes glowing red with rage.

"No!" Evelyn screamed, reaching out desperately as the darkness dragged him away. "Don't let it take you!"

The fireflies flared one last time, their light bursting through the clearing, but it wasn't enough. The shadows engulfed him, and he disappeared into the darkness, leaving Evelyn standing alone in the fading light.

The barrier collapsed, and the fireflies dimmed, their light flickering weakly as the energy drained from the forest. Eldrin, Tristan, and Lila rushed to Evelyn's side, their faces etched with concern.

"We have to go," Eldrin said, his voice filled with urgency. "The darkness is too strong here. We can't stay."

Evelyn shook her head, tears streaming down her face. "I was so close. I almost had him…"

Tristan gently took her arm, pulling her away from the center of the clearing. "We'll find another way," he said softly. "But we have to get out of here. The forest won't hold the darkness back for long."

Lila placed a comforting hand on Evelyn's shoulder. "We're not giving up. We'll find him again. We'll save him."

Evelyn nodded, though her heart felt heavy with the weight of the failure. She had seen him—truly seen him—but the darkness had taken him once more. And now, as they retreated from the clearing, she knew that the battle for his soul was far from over.

Chapter 23: "Echoes of the Past"

The forest was alive with secrets. The fireflies danced ahead in a winding pattern, guiding Evelyn, Lila, Tristan, and Eldrin through the labyrinth of towering trees. The further they ventured, the more the atmosphere shifted—cold, damp air clung to their skin, and the once vibrant hues of the forest faded into lifeless grays.

Eldrin led the way, his sharp eyes scanning the surroundings, but even he seemed unsettled by the unnatural stillness. It was as if the entire forest was holding its breath. Every rustle, every crack of a twig, made them flinch, wondering if something was watching, lurking just beyond their sight.

"Do you hear that?" Tristan murmured, slowing his pace. His hand hovered near the hilt of his dagger.

They all stopped, straining their ears. There was nothing—no birds, no wind—only an eerie hum, like distant whispers carried on a forgotten breeze. It was faint, almost imperceptible, but it set Evelyn's nerves on edge.

"Keep moving," Eldrin said under his breath, though his voice lacked its usual confidence.

As they pressed on, the fireflies suddenly veered off the path, leading them to a small clearing. In the center stood a large stone altar, half buried under thick layers of moss and creeping vines. It was ancient, worn by centuries of weather and decay, yet it exuded a strange, almost magnetic energy.

"Here," Lila whispered, pointing at the altar. "This is where they've brought us."

Evelyn's heart pounded as she approached the stone, her eyes drawn to something resting atop it—a scroll, old and fragile, with edges that seemed to disintegrate in the slightest breeze. Carefully, she lifted it, feeling a strange connection as her fingers brushed the parchment. The symbols carved into the stone and scrawled on the scroll were familiar, though she couldn't recall why.

She glanced at Eldrin, whose gaze was fixed on the scroll with a mix of wariness and fascination. "These markings... They're the same as before," she muttered, her fingers tracing the symbols. "I've seen them."

Without waiting for a response, Evelyn unrolled the scroll, revealing faded, ancient writing beneath the strange glyphs. Her breath caught in her throat as the words came into focus, and a memory stirred deep within her.

"These words..." she began, almost in a trance. "They're... from one of my poems."

Eldrin's eyes widened, and the others gathered closer. The fireflies hovered around them, their light casting eerie shadows over the altar. Slowly, Evelyn began to read aloud:

"Whispers Through the Veil"
"In shadows deep, where time does break,
Love lingers on, for hearts to ache.
Beyond the veil, a whisper calls,
Through endless night, the darkness falls..."

Her voice faltered as the words seemed to come alive, resonating with the forest itself. The trees groaned, and a low hum vibrated through the ground beneath their feet. Tristan and Lila exchanged anxious glances, but Evelyn kept reading:

"A love once lost, now bound in chains,
Through heartache's grip, the dark remains.
Yet whispers guide those who dare see,
The veil may tear, and hearts set free..."

As she finished, a gust of wind blew through the clearing, though the air had been completely still before. The fireflies scattered momentarily, their light flickering wildly, as though reacting to the words. The forest, which had been eerily silent, now buzzed with a low, ominous hum.

Eldrin stepped forward, his brow furrowed. "These aren't just words... This is more than poetry."

"There's magic in it," Evelyn replied, her voice barely a whisper. "A warning... or a clue."

Tristan shook his head, uneasy. "What does it mean? Love lost, bound in chains? Could it be referring to the ancient evil?"

Lila was already studying the symbols etched into the stone altar, her fingers tracing them cautiously. "It's as if the poem is connected to the forest itself. Could it be... tied to Evelyn's past?"

Evelyn's heart raced. Her connection to the ancient evil had always felt personal, but now it seemed deeper than she had imagined. The poem wasn't just a vague prophecy—it was a piece of her story. A love, once lost, now bound in chains. The words echoed in her mind like a ghost's whisper.

She looked up at Eldrin, whose expression was grim. "It's tied to love, and loss," she said, her voice trembling. "I think... the ancient evil feeds on it. It thrives on brokenness, on the grief of what was once cherished."

Eldrin nodded slowly, piecing it together. "The forest was corrupted by something more than just darkness. It was twisted by emotion—by love that was twisted and lost."

Lila's eyes widened in realization. "Then perhaps the way to weaken it lies not in brute force, but in the heart. Maybe... love can still be its undoing."

Evelyn wasn't so sure. The poem had spoken of hearts set free, but how could they free something that had been lost to the darkness for so long? She glanced at the scroll, now resting in her hands, and felt a deep sense of foreboding. The fireflies hovered closer, their light dimming as though warning them of what lay ahead.

"We should move," Eldrin said firmly, his gaze sweeping the clearing. "This scroll is important, but it's only a piece of the puzzle. There's more we need to uncover."

Reluctantly, Evelyn tucked the scroll into her satchel, but she couldn't shake the feeling that the answers they sought were more dangerous than any of them had realized. The ancient evil wasn't just a force—they were up against something far more personal. And it was waiting for them.

The fireflies began to move again, this time leading them deeper into the forest. As they followed, the darkness seemed to close in around them, the whispers growing louder. The air grew thick with tension, and the shadows between the trees seemed to shift and stir, as if alive with a malevolent presence.

Evelyn walked in silence, her mind heavy with the weight of the poem's meaning. The ancient evil was tied to love—but whose? And how could they defeat something that fed on the very emotions that had once given life meaning?

The forest seemed to swallow them whole as they ventured deeper into its dark heart. The fireflies hovered like tiny embers in the air, guiding their path through the thickening shadows. The towering trees, once full of life, now loomed over them like twisted sentinels, their branches clawing at the sky.

Evelyn's thoughts lingered on the scroll tucked safely in her satchel. The weight of the words felt heavy on her chest. It wasn't just the cryptic warning, or the realization that love and loss were intertwined with the ancient evil—they were walking straight into its lair. And something, deep inside her, was stirring.

"We should stop soon," Tristan said, breaking the silence. "We don't know how far this goes, and the fireflies are slowing down."

Eldrin glanced ahead, his eyes following the fireflies as they flickered and dimmed. "They're cautious. They sense something."

Lila shuddered. "I can feel it too. The air is colder, heavier. Something's wrong here."

They pressed on for a few more minutes until the fireflies slowed to a near halt. They hovered near a small outcropping of rocks, where the ground dipped into a natural hollow, surrounded by a ring of twisted, ancient trees. The clearing was unsettling, but it offered some protection.

"We'll stop here," Eldrin said, already surveying the area. "We'll need to rest, gather our thoughts, and figure out what the next move is."

The group settled in, though the unease in the air was palpable. Tristan started a small fire using dry branches and flint, and the faint warmth was a welcome comfort against the chilling forest. Evelyn sat near the flames, her eyes drawn to the distant shadows beyond their camp. She could hear the faintest whispers—so soft she couldn't be sure if they were real or in her mind.

"What do you think the poem meant?" Lila asked, her voice low as she joined Evelyn by the fire. "About love and loss... how does that connect to the ancient evil?"

Evelyn shook her head slowly. "I'm not sure. But I feel like... it's more than just a metaphor. It's almost as if the evil itself is sustained by those emotions."

Lila frowned. "But why love? What does it have to gain by feeding on something like that?"

Evelyn's thoughts raced back to her ex-lover, the man she once thought was lost to her forever. Could it be that his fate, whatever dark twist had befallen him, was connected to this evil? The thought sent a cold shiver through her spine. She hadn't spoken much about him to the others, and now that she was piecing things together, it felt even more dangerous to reveal the truth.

"I don't know," Evelyn replied, avoiding Lila's gaze. "But whatever it is, it's powerful. It's feeding on something we can't see."

Eldrin, who had been pacing near the edge of the camp, turned to them, his expression unreadable. "I think Evelyn is right," he said quietly. "Love, in its truest form, can be both a strength and a weakness. The ancient evil knows that. It's been manipulating those emotions, twisting them into something dark."

Tristan, sharpening his blade near the fire, looked up. "So what? Are we supposed to defeat it by... love? That seems impossible."

Eldrin's gaze shifted to the darkened forest. "Maybe not by love, but by understanding how it has been corrupted. The poem speaks of hearts bound in chains—perhaps there is a way to free those chains, to break whatever hold this evil has over the emotions it has twisted."

Evelyn's heart skipped a beat. The idea that love could be the key both terrified and intrigued her. But could she confront the ancient evil without confronting the pain of her past?

Suddenly, a low growl echoed from the depths of the forest. Everyone froze, their eyes snapping to the source of the sound. It was distant, but unmistakable—a deep, rumbling growl that reverberated through the trees.

"The creature..." Lila whispered, standing slowly, her hand resting on the hilt of her sword.

Eldrin moved swiftly, his bow already drawn. "It's coming."

The fireflies flickered, their light dimming as if warning them of the impending danger. Evelyn rose to her feet, her pulse quickening. The growl grew louder, closer. Whatever was out there, it wasn't hiding anymore.

Tristan, already on his feet, moved to Evelyn's side. "We need to move. We can't fight it here."

But before anyone could react, the ground beneath them trembled. The fire crackled and sparked, and the air grew colder still. From the shadows beyond the clearing, a massive figure emerged—its form a twisted mass of darkness, with glowing red eyes that pierced the night. The creature was monstrous, unlike anything they had ever seen, and its very presence seemed to drain the warmth from the air.

The fireflies swarmed, circling frantically around the creature, but it didn't flinch. It let out a deafening roar, sending a shockwave through the clearing that nearly knocked them off their feet.

"Go!" Eldrin shouted, nocking an arrow and loosing it at the beast. The arrow struck, but it barely slowed the creature down.

Evelyn grabbed the scroll from her satchel, instinctively clutching it to her chest as the creature advanced. Her mind raced—there had to be something in the poem, some hint she had missed. Something to stop this nightmare.

She glanced at the symbols on the scroll, her eyes widening as realization dawned. The poem wasn't just a warning—it was a key. The symbols weren't just letters—they were instructions. A way to bind the creature, to stop its advance.

"Evelyn, now!" Lila shouted, readying her sword as the creature lunged toward them.

Without thinking, Evelyn raised the scroll high, chanting the words that came to her mind. The symbols glowed faintly, and for a brief moment, the creature hesitated. The fireflies swarmed it, their light intensifying, and the beast roared in frustration as it was held back by some unseen force.

But Evelyn knew it wouldn't last long. The scroll was only buying them time.

"Run!" she yelled, her voice cracking with urgency. "We need to find the source of the magic—the altar. It's the only way!"

Together, they fled the clearing, the fireflies guiding their way. The creature's enraged roars echoed behind them, but they didn't stop. They couldn't. The truth of the ancient evil was within reach—but only if they could survive long enough to uncover it.

Chapter 24: "The Altar of Shadows"

The forest was a blur as Evelyn, Lila, Tristan, and Eldrin ran, their breath ragged and hearts pounding. The creature's roars echoed behind them, growing fainter with each step, but they knew it was only a matter of time before it regained its strength and resumed the chase. The fireflies darted ahead, their frantic movements guiding the group deeper into the forest's twisted labyrinth.

Evelyn's mind raced along with her pulse. The symbols on the scroll—there was something familiar about them. Something deeper. She clutched the scroll tightly, the worn parchment crinkling in her hand. Every time she glanced down at the faintly glowing runes, she felt a pull—a connection she couldn't quite explain. The poem she had read was only the beginning. The scroll held secrets yet to be uncovered, but time was slipping away.

"We're getting close," Eldrin called out from the front, his voice low and urgent. "I can feel it."

Lila nodded, keeping pace beside him. "The air... it's different. Heavier."

The fireflies slowed their frantic pace, leading the group into a small, enclosed clearing. At the center of the clearing stood a stone altar, much like the one they had encountered earlier, but this one was different. The air around it shimmered with a faint, almost imperceptible glow, and strange runes were etched into its surface. Ancient symbols like those on the scroll, but far more intricate, covered every inch of the stone.

"This is it," Evelyn breathed, her voice barely above a whisper. She could feel the weight of the magic surrounding the altar. It was as though the very air was alive, pulsing with power.

Eldrin approached the altar cautiously, his hand hovering above the stone. "This altar... it's older than anything I've seen. The magic here is ancient."

Tristan circled the clearing, keeping an eye on the surrounding forest. The creature was still out there, lurking, and he didn't trust that it wouldn't return. "We need to hurry. Whatever we're going to do, we need to do it fast."

Evelyn nodded, stepping closer to the altar. The symbols on the scroll began to glow brighter as she neared the stone, pulsing in rhythm with the runes carved into the altar's surface. She laid the scroll out flat on the stone, aligning the symbols with those etched into the stone.

For a moment, nothing happened.

Then, with a low hum, the altar began to vibrate, the runes glowing a brilliant gold. The fireflies, hovering just above the stone, shimmered with light as if in response. A soft wind stirred the air, and the entire forest seemed to hold its breath.

Evelyn's hands trembled as she placed her palms on the stone, feeling the raw power coursing through it. She could hear the whispers again, louder this time, clearer. They echoed in her mind, fragments of a forgotten voice. Her voice. The words of the poem came rushing back, but now they carried weight, meaning beyond the ink on the page.

"In shadows deep, where time does break,

Love lingers on, for hearts to ache..."

As she recited the lines, the wind grew stronger, swirling around the clearing. The runes on the altar flared with light, and the ground beneath them trembled. Eldrin, Lila, and Tristan exchanged nervous glances but remained silent, watching as the magic unfolded before them.

"A love once lost, now bound in chains,

Through heartache's grip, the dark remains..."

The fireflies gathered above the altar, their glow intensifying until they were a swirling mass of light. Evelyn could feel the connection growing stronger, the magic of the forest intertwining with the words of the poem, with the emotions buried deep within her heart. The ancient evil wasn't just feeding on love—it had been born from it, twisted by pain and loss.

Evelyn's breath hitched as the final line of the poem escaped her lips:

"Yet whispers guide those who dare see,

The veil may tear, and hearts set free."

With a deafening crack, the altar split open, revealing a hidden compartment beneath the stone. Inside lay a shimmering shard of obsidian, black as night and pulsing with dark energy. The air around it was thick with malevolence, and Evelyn instinctively recoiled.

"That's it," Eldrin said, his voice strained. "That's the heart of the ancient evil."

Lila's eyes narrowed. "We destroy it, and we destroy the evil."

Tristan took a step forward, eyeing the shard warily. "But how? We can't just smash it. There's something more to this."

Evelyn's heart raced as she reached for the shard. The moment her fingers brushed its surface, her mind was flooded with images—visions of the past, of the forest before it had fallen into darkness. She saw herself, standing with her ex-lover, his face shadowed but unmistakably familiar. They had been happy once, but something had changed. The love they had shared had turned to bitterness, to regret. And from that pain, the darkness had grown.

She staggered back, her hand trembling. "It's not just the forest," she whispered. "The ancient evil... it's tied to him. To my past. Our love—it was broken. And this darkness, it's feeding on that brokenness."

Eldrin's eyes narrowed. "Then we need to sever that connection. If the evil is tied to your love, then there must be a way to break it."

Evelyn's mind raced as she pieced it together. The poem had spoken of hearts bound in chains—chains of regret, of lost love. But if those chains could be broken, if the love that had been twisted could be set free...

"There's a way," she said, her voice steadying. "But it won't be easy. I need to confront him—what's left of him. The part of him that's still consumed by the darkness. If I can reach him, if I can remind him of the love we once had..."

Lila frowned. "You're talking about facing the ancient evil head-on."

Evelyn nodded. "Yes. And I'm the only one who can do it."

Tristan shook his head. "That's too dangerous. You saw what that thing did back there. It's not just him anymore—it's something far worse."

"I know," Evelyn said softly. "But it's the only way. I have to try."

Eldrin placed a hand on her shoulder, his expression grim but resolute. "We'll be with you. Whatever happens, you won't face it alone."

Evelyn met his gaze and nodded. She knew the risks, but she also knew there was no other choice. The fireflies circled above, their glow bright and steady, as if guiding her toward the inevitable confrontation.

The ancient evil awaited them, and with it, the answers to everything that had been lost in the shadows of the past.

Chapter 26: "The Broken Heart of Lucian"

The darkness surged around Evelyn as she ran, the fireflies flickering dimly ahead, guiding her through the suffocating void. Behind her, she could hear the roar of the ancient evil, echoing in the space between worlds. Lucian's voice, full of pain and hatred, reverberated in her mind, but she couldn't turn back—not yet.

The forest around her felt alive, shifting and moving with each step she took. The trees twisted and bent, their branches reaching for her like skeletal hands. Shadows danced at the edges of her vision, watching, waiting. Every breath was a struggle, the air thick with the weight of the ancient magic that pulsed through the ground beneath her feet.

She clutched the scroll tightly in her hand, the symbols glowing faintly in the darkness. They were her only hope, the only thing that could save Lucian from the darkness that had consumed him. But with every step, her resolve faltered. Could she really save him? Or was he already lost to the ancient evil, beyond her reach?

Ahead, the fireflies stopped, their light dimming as they hovered in a tight circle. Evelyn slowed to a stop, her heart racing as she approached the glowing insects. In the center of the clearing, the earth split open, revealing a jagged chasm of darkness that seemed to pulse with a malevolent energy. The fireflies circled the chasm, their light flickering as if in warning.

Evelyn's breath caught in her throat as she stepped closer to the edge. The air around her grew colder, and the whispers of the forest grew louder, echoing in her ears. From the depths of the chasm, a figure slowly emerged, shrouded in shadow and smoke.

Lucian.

His form was barely recognizable, his once-human features twisted by the darkness that clung to him like a second skin. His eyes glowed with a cold, red light, filled with rage and sorrow. The air around him crackled with dark energy, and the ground trembled beneath his feet.

Evelyn's heart ached at the sight of him. This wasn't the man she had once loved. This was a shadow of the man, a twisted reflection of what he had become. But somewhere, deep beneath the darkness, she knew the real Lucian was still there, trapped and broken.

"Lucian," she whispered, her voice trembling. "I'm sorry. I'm so sorry."

His eyes flickered, but the hatred in them remained. "Sorry?" His voice was low, guttural, filled with bitterness. "You left me to die, Evelyn. You left me, and this... this is what I became."

Tears welled in Evelyn's eyes, but she forced herself to remain steady. "I made a mistake. I know that now. But I never meant for this to happen. I never wanted you to suffer."

Lucian stepped closer, his movements slow, deliberate. The darkness around him pulsed, and the air grew heavier with each step he took. "You didn't care then, did you? You betrayed me. You left me for someone else."

Evelyn flinched at the accusation. She could still remember the night it had all gone wrong—the guilt, the regret that had eaten away at her since. But this was more than just about their past. The ancient evil had twisted Lucian's pain, turning his heartbreak into something far more dangerous.

"I was wrong, Lucian," she said, her voice thick with emotion. "I was selfish, and I hurt you. But I didn't know—didn't realize—what it would lead to."

Lucian's eyes narrowed, the hatred in them burning brighter. "No. You knew what you were doing. You knew it would destroy me."

Evelyn's hands trembled as she clutched the scroll tighter, the symbols glowing faintly in the darkness. She could feel the ancient magic stirring within the scroll, waiting to be unleashed. But she didn't want to use it—not yet. Not if there was still a chance to reach him.

"I never wanted to destroy you," she whispered. "I loved you, Lucian. And I still do."

For a moment, the darkness around him seemed to falter. His eyes softened, and she saw a flicker of the man she had once known—the man who had loved her so deeply, so fiercely. But just as quickly, the darkness surged again, wrapping around him like a suffocating shroud.

"You loved me?" he spat, his voice venomous. "If you had loved me, you wouldn't have left me to die. You wouldn't have driven me to this!" He gestured to the chasm, the shadows swirling around him. "I tried to escape the pain, Evelyn. I tried to end it all. But instead, this forest... it took me. It consumed me. And now I'm bound to it. Forever."

Evelyn's heart shattered at his words. She could see the pain in his eyes, the overwhelming sorrow that had driven him to the edge of despair. And she knew that beneath all the hatred, all the darkness, that pain still ruled him.

"I should have been there for you," she said, her voice barely a whisper. "I should have fought for us. But it's not too late, Lucian. We can still fight this. Together."

Lucian shook his head, his expression twisted with anger and grief. "There is no 'together' anymore, Evelyn. There's only darkness. And it's too late for me. The forest owns me now."

The air around them grew colder, the shadows thickening as the ancient evil stirred, sensing the conflict within Lucian. Evelyn could feel the weight of the darkness pressing down on her, trying to drown her in despair. But she refused to give in.

"No," she said, her voice firm. "It's not too late. I know you're still in there, Lucian. I know you can fight this."

The shadows around Lucian writhed, coiling around his body like living chains. His eyes flashed with pain, and for a moment, the darkness seemed to retreat. But then it surged again, more powerful than before, and Lucian let out a cry of agony.

"I can't!" he shouted, his voice raw with pain. "I can't fight it!"

"Yes, you can," Evelyn said, stepping closer. "You're stronger than this. We're stronger than this."

Lucian's eyes met hers, and for a fleeting moment, she saw the man she had loved—the man who had once been her everything. But the darkness was relentless, and it wasn't willing to let him go.

With a roar, the ancient evil erupted from the chasm, a mass of shadows and malevolent energy. It surged toward Evelyn, its tendrils reaching for her like claws. But before it could reach her, Lucian stepped in front of her, his body trembling as he fought to hold the darkness back.

"Go!" he shouted, his voice strained. "I can't... hold it much longer."

Evelyn's heart ached as she watched him struggle against the darkness. She knew he was giving everything he had to protect her, but she also knew that he couldn't hold on forever.

"No," she whispered, her voice breaking. "I'm not leaving you."

The scroll in her hand glowed brighter, the symbols pulsing with ancient magic. She could feel the power within it, waiting to be unleashed. But she hesitated. If she used the scroll, if she invoked its magic, it might destroy Lucian along with the ancient evil. And that was a risk she wasn't willing to take.

Tears streamed down her face as she reached out to him, her hand brushing against his. "Lucian, please... don't do this."

Lucian's eyes met hers, and for a brief moment, the hatred in them faded. He opened his mouth to speak, but before he could, the darkness surged again, swallowing him whole.

Evelyn screamed as the ancient evil consumed him, its tendrils of shadow wrapping around his body like chains. The ground beneath them trembled, and the air crackled with dark energy.

And then, everything went still.

The shadows receded, leaving only silence in their wake. Lucian was gone, swallowed by the darkness that had claimed him. And Evelyn was left standing alone, her heart shattered, the scroll glowing faintly in her hand.

She had lost him. Again.

Chapter 27: "Tears of the Forest"

Evelyn stood frozen, her breath shallow as the final remnants of Lucian disappeared into the shadows. The ancient evil had taken him—again. Her hands trembled, the scroll in her grip barely glowing now, its ancient power flickering like a dying flame. The weight of it all pressed down on her like a heavy shroud, and for the first time in her journey, she felt utterly helpless.

The forest around her was eerily still. Even the fireflies, who had faithfully guided her, dimmed their light as though in mourning. The once vibrant energy that had filled the air was gone, replaced by an oppressive silence.

Tears welled in her eyes, blurring her vision. She tried to blink them away, but the flood was unstoppable. The pain of losing Lucian—of failing him again—overwhelmed her. It was too much. The guilt, the regret, the sorrow. It all poured out, no longer contained within the walls she had built around her heart.

She sank to her knees, her head bowed, and the first tear fell to the earth. It hit the forest floor like a raindrop, but the impact rippled outward, resonating with the ancient magic that still lingered in the ground.

Her voice trembled as she spoke the words of the poem that had been haunting her for so long, the words that had once been a reflection of her pain, but now felt like a prophecy fulfilled:

"Tears"

"Tears fall like rain upon the soul,
Washing away all hope, leaving only cold.

In the silence of the heart, they call,
Echoes of the past, of love's cruel fall."

Each word felt like a dagger to her heart. The tears came faster now, slipping down her cheeks as she remembered the love they had shared, and how it had all crumbled into nothing. Lucian's face flashed in her mind—his smile, his laugh, the warmth in his eyes before everything had gone wrong.

She had failed him. Again.

"They carve their path down weary faces,
Tracing lines of grief, of lost embraces.
Each drop a memory, a wound left wide,
A love forsaken, a heart denied."

The poem's words hung in the air, mingling with the ancient magic of the forest. The fireflies pulsed faintly, their light flickering like dying stars. The forest seemed to echo her grief, the trees swaying gently as though they, too, mourned with her.

Evelyn's shoulders shook as she wept, her sobs quiet in the vast silence of the forest. She had come so far, fought so hard, but in the end, it had all been for nothing. The darkness had won. Lucian was gone.

"Yet in these tears, a truth may lie,
In every drop, a whisper, a cry.
For love does not fade, though hearts may break,
And from the pain, new hope may wake."

She wiped at her eyes, the tears blurring her vision. The words of the poem—her poem—resonated deep within her. Could there still be hope? Could there still be a way to save Lucian, to break the hold the ancient evil had over him?

Her fingers tightened around the scroll, the symbols faint but still pulsing with a lingering magic. The fireflies, though dim, hadn't abandoned her. They hovered close, their light soft but steady, like a heartbeat in the darkness.

Eldrin's voice broke through the silence, soft but firm. "Evelyn."

She didn't look up. The weight of her sorrow was too great, her failure too fresh. But he knelt beside her, his hand resting gently on her shoulder.

"We're not done," he said, his voice filled with quiet determination. "There's still a chance. There's always a chance."

Evelyn sniffed, her tears slowing but still falling. "I've lost him, Eldrin. I tried, but the darkness... it's taken him."

Eldrin's grip tightened on her shoulder, his presence a steadying force. "You haven't lost him yet. As long as there's breath in your body, as long as you're willing to fight, there's still hope."

The fireflies circled above them, their light growing slightly brighter. Evelyn wiped at her eyes, the words of her poem still echoing in her mind. She wanted to believe Eldrin, to believe that there was still a way to save Lucian, to undo the damage that had been done.

But could she?

She stood slowly, her knees weak, but her resolve beginning to return. She wasn't ready to give up. Not yet. The tears had washed away her despair, leaving behind a faint flicker of hope.

"We need to find the source of the evil," Evelyn said, her voice stronger than before. "There has to be something... some way to break the hold it has on him."

Eldrin nodded, standing beside her. "Then we keep moving. We find the source, and we end this."

Evelyn looked up at the fireflies, their light now shining brighter. She could feel the pull of the forest, the ancient magic guiding her once again. Lucian wasn't lost. Not completely. And she wasn't going to stop until she had done everything she could to save him.

The fireflies began to move, leading them deeper into the forest, toward the heart of the ancient evil. Evelyn wiped the last of her tears from her cheeks, her heart heavy but determined.

This wasn't over.

Chapter 28: "The Tree of Sorrows"

The forest was darker than ever as Evelyn, Eldrin, Lila, and Tristan followed the faint light of the fireflies deeper into the forest's heart. The air was thick with an unsettling quiet, broken only by the faint rustling of leaves and the occasional creak of ancient branches overhead.

Evelyn's breath hitched as the fireflies slowed, their light dimming. Before them stood a massive tree, its bark blackened and twisted, its roots stretching deep into the ground like skeletal fingers. The air around It was dense, almost suffocating, as if the tree itself was alive with the weight of the sorrows it had collected over centuries.

"This is the Tree of Sorrows," Eldrin whispered, his voice filled with quiet reverence. "A place where broken souls leave their final words."

Evelyn stared at the tree, her heart heavy. She could feel the presence of Lucian, a deep sadness woven into the very air around the tree. She knew without a doubt that he had been here. This was where the darkness had claimed him fully.

Her eyes scanned the bark of the tree, which was covered in carvings—names, symbols, and verses etched into the wood by those who had lost everything. But it wasn't the carvings that caught her attention. Near the base of the tree, pinned beneath a shard of broken stone, was a piece of paper. Faded, weathered, but still intact.

With trembling hands, Evelyn knelt and gently lifted the paper. Her heart pounded as she unfolded it, recognizing Lucian's handwriting. The words scrawled across the page sent a shiver down her spine. It was a poem, one that Lucian had left behind for her—a final expression of his heartbreak.

She swallowed hard and began to read aloud:
"Heartbreak Lullaby"
Hush now, heart, don't make a sound,
The pieces fall, they hit the ground.
Love that lived inside my chest
Is now a ghost that won't find rest.

Her voice wavered, and tears pricked at the corners of her eyes. Lucian's pain was palpable in every word. She could feel it, deep in her chest—the heartbreak that had consumed him, that had driven him into the arms of the ancient evil.

Your voice, a song I can't forget,
But every note drips with regret.
I cling to words you never said,
Now lullabies hum with the dead.

Evelyn's breath hitched as she continued. The regret in the poem mirrored her own. She had never realized how deeply her betrayal had scarred him, how it had become the very thing that drove him to his despair. And now, the ancient evil had twisted that heartbreak into something dark, something relentless.

Tears carve rivers down my skin,
You slipped away, I held you in.
A silence screams where love once bloomed,
Now darkness fills an empty room.

Her voice broke, and she had to stop to compose herself. The imagery of love turning to silence, of a room once filled with warmth now cold and empty, hit her hard. She had lived that silence, that emptiness, ever since Lucian had been taken by the forest.

So close your eyes, and drift away,
The night will steal what's left of day.
I sing this pain, though love has died—

This is my last heartbreak lullaby.

When she finished reading, the forest seemed to hold its breath. The fireflies flickered faintly, their light reflecting off the tears that streamed down Evelyn's face. She clutched the poem to her chest, her heart aching with the weight of Lucian's final words.

He had left this for her, a parting gift wrapped in sorrow. It was a testament to the love they had once shared, but also to the pain that had consumed him. He hadn't just lost her—he had lost himself.

Eldrin stepped closer, his gaze somber. "He left this behind for you. But there's more here than just grief, Evelyn. There's still a spark of the man you loved inside him."

Evelyn wiped her tears, her hand shaking as she folded the poem and tucked it into her satchel. "But how do I bring him back? How do I fight the darkness that has taken him?"

Eldrin's expression was grim. "We destroy the source of the ancient evil. Only then will Lucian have a chance to break free."

Evelyn nodded, though her heart felt heavy with uncertainty. The poem had made it clear that Lucian had accepted his fate, but she wasn't ready to give up on him. Not yet.

"I need to find him," she whispered. "I need to tell him that I haven't given up."

Eldrin rested a hand on her shoulder. "We'll find him, and we'll face whatever comes. But first, we need to reach the heart of the darkness."

Evelyn took a deep breath, steadying herself. The poem lingered in her mind, its words like a lullaby of sorrow, but they also fueled her determination. Lucian wasn't lost—not completely. There was still a chance to save him, to bring him back from the edge of despair.

The fireflies began to move again, leading them away from the Tree of Sorrows and deeper into the forest's shadows. The path ahead was dark, but Evelyn's resolve had never been stronger. She would fight for Lucian, no matter the cost.

And as they pressed forward, the last lines of the poem echoed in her mind—a reminder of the love that had once been, and the hope that still lingered, faint but unyielding.

Chapter 29: "The Fire Within"

The forest air crackled with tension, thick and oppressive, as if the ancient magic itself was pressing down on Evelyn's chest. The words of Lucian's poem, "Heartbreak Lullaby," echoed in her mind, filling her with grief and a mounting rage that was impossible to contain.

She stood in front of the Tree of Sorrows, her heart pounding as her emotions twisted into a storm she couldn't control. The tree—dark, gnarled, and ancient—seemed to mock her, a monument to everything she had lost. It had seen Lucian's final moments of humanity, had swallowed his sorrow, and now stood as a silent reminder of her betrayal.

Her fists clenched at her sides as the fire of regret and fury burned within her. The weight of her mistakes—her betrayal—crushed her under a wave of guilt that made it hard to breathe. She had destroyed everything, and now Lucian was lost to the darkness because of her.

"I have to destroy it," Evelyn muttered under her breath, her voice trembling with anger. "This tree... it took him. It took everything."

She turned to Lila, her eyes wild, and snatched the torch from her hand.

"Evelyn, wait!" Lila called, but Evelyn was already moving toward the tree.

With the torch blazing in her hand, she stormed forward, her heart racing. The flames cast long, flickering shadows on the bark, illuminating the names and verses carved into its surface by those who had come before her. But all she could see, all she could feel, was

Lucian's pain. His heartbreak. The love that had died because of her betrayal.

"I'll end this," Evelyn snarled, her voice thick with rage. "I'll burn it all down."

The torch flared in her hand as she raised it toward the tree. Her body trembled with the force of her fury, the fire within her threatening to consume her as much as the flames would consume the tree.

But before she could bring the torch down, a firm hand caught her wrist, stopping her mid-swing.

"Evelyn, no!" Eldrin's voice was sharp, filled with urgency. He stepped in front of her, gripping her wrist tightly, his eyes locked on hers. "You can't do this."

Evelyn struggled against his hold, her breath coming in ragged gasps. "Why not?" she spat, her voice choked with emotion. "This tree... it took him! It took everything from me!"

Eldrin held her wrist steady, his voice softening. "This tree didn't take him, Evelyn. The darkness did. Burning this tree won't bring him back. It won't undo the past."

Tears welled in Evelyn's eyes as the weight of her grief pressed down on her. "But I hurt him, Eldrin. I betrayed him. He loved me, and I destroyed him. This tree—this cursed place—it's a monument to everything I've lost. I have to do something. I have to make this right."

Eldrin's gaze softened, his grip on her wrist loosening slightly. "I know you're in pain. But this tree is not the cause of the evil. It's a marker, a reminder of those who have been lost to it. If you destroy it, you destroy the memories of those who left their sorrow here—including Lucian. His poem, his final words, are a part of this place. Destroying the tree won't free him."

Evelyn's grip on the torch faltered, her arm trembling as Eldrin's words sank in. She looked at the tree again, at the carvings etched into its bark, the verses of loss and pain left behind by those who had suffered as she had. And then her eyes fell on the piece of paper—the poem Lucian had left for her.

"Heartbreak Lullaby" had been his final goodbye, a testament to the love they had once shared and the heartbreak that had consumed him. It was a piece of him, a piece of their past, left here for her to find. Destroying the tree would mean destroying that part of him, too.

The torch slipped from her hand, falling to the ground with a dull thud as the flame flickered out. Sobs wracked her body, and she sank to her knees before the tree, her face buried in her hands.

"I don't know what to do," she whispered, her voice breaking. "I've lost him. I destroyed everything."

Eldrin knelt beside her, his hand resting on her shoulder. "You haven't lost him yet, Evelyn. As long as you're still willing to fight, there's hope. Redemption doesn't come from burning the past—it comes from fighting for the future."

Evelyn's shoulders shook with the force of her grief, her tears falling freely. "But how do I save him? How do I earn his forgiveness after everything I've done?"

Eldrin's grip tightened, his voice calm but firm. "You fight for him. You show him that you're willing to do whatever it takes to make things right. You fight the darkness, Evelyn, not with rage but with love."

Evelyn wiped at her tears, her heart aching with the weight of her regret. She had made a terrible mistake—betraying Lucian in a moment of weakness—but Eldrin was right. She couldn't change the past. She couldn't undo what had happened. But she could fight for the future. She could fight for Lucian, for his forgiveness, for redemption.

With a deep, shuddering breath, Evelyn rose to her feet. Her body trembled with exhaustion, but her mind was clearer than it had been since Lucian's fall. She couldn't let her anger destroy what little hope remained. She had to be stronger than the rage and guilt that threatened to consume her.

"We need to find him," Evelyn said, her voice steadying. "We need to destroy the source of the ancient evil. Only then will Lucian have a chance."

Eldrin nodded and stood beside her, offering his hand. "Then let's go. We still have a long way to go, but we're not alone."

Evelyn took his hand, her heart heavy but her resolve renewed. She glanced one last time at the Tree of Sorrows, the place where Lucian's pain had been left behind in the form of his poem. She wouldn't forget it, wouldn't let his heartbreak be the end of their story.

As the fireflies began to move, flickering like small stars in the darkness, Evelyn followed. The path ahead was uncertain, but she was ready. She had to be. The ancient evil waited for them, and Lucian was out there—lost in the shadows.

And she was going to bring him back.

Chapter 30: "The Path to Redemption"

The air was colder, sharper, as Evelyn, Eldrin, Lila, and Tristan ventured deeper into the heart of the forest. The fireflies flickered weakly, their glow barely cutting through the oppressive darkness that pressed in on all sides. Every step felt like a battle against the forest itself—against the ancient evil that had twisted its roots and branches into something malevolent, something alive.

But it wasn't the forest that made Evelyn's heart race—it was what lay ahead. Lucian. The man she had loved, the man she had betrayed, the man she had lost to the darkness.

Her mind raced, replaying the last time she had seen him. His eyes, once full of warmth and affection, had been cold and distant, filled with anger and hurt. The darkness had consumed him, fed off the pain she had caused. But beneath the shadows, she had seen a flicker of the man he had once been. The man she was determined to save.

"I don't know if I can do this," Evelyn whispered, her voice barely audible in the gloom. She felt Lila's presence beside her, a comforting anchor in the sea of her doubt.

"You can," Lila said firmly, her voice cutting through the fog of Evelyn's uncertainty. "You've come this far. You can't give up now."

Evelyn's heart ached with the weight of her guilt. "But what if it's too late? What if the darkness has taken him completely? What if he hates me too much to ever forgive me?"

Lila was silent for a moment, choosing her words carefully. "Maybe he does. Maybe he doesn't. But you have to try. You owe him that much."

Evelyn nodded, her throat tight with emotion. She did owe Lucian that much. She owed him everything. She had broken his heart, destroyed the trust they had built, and now she had to face the consequences. But she wasn't just fighting for forgiveness—she was fighting to save his soul.

Ahead, the fireflies stopped, hovering in a tight circle around a large stone altar. The air around it hummed with dark energy, a low, throbbing pulse that made the hairs on Evelyn's arms stand on end. This was it—the source of the ancient evil, the place where the darkness had taken root.

"This is it," Eldrin said quietly, stepping forward. "The heart of the forest's curse."

Evelyn's breath hitched as she followed, her eyes locked on the altar. She could feel Lucian's presence—his pain, his anger—woven into the very air around her. He was here. She was certain of it.

Her hands trembled as she reached for the scroll in her satchel, the ancient symbols glowing faintly as if in response to the dark energy around them. She could feel the power within the scroll, but she wasn't sure if it would be enough.

The ground trembled beneath their feet, and from the shadows, a figure stepped forward.

Lucian.

Evelyn's breath caught in her throat. He was different from the last time she had seen him. His once-human form was now wreathed in shadows, the darkness twisting around him like living chains. His eyes, glowing with a cold, red light, were empty of the warmth they had once held. The man she had loved was buried beneath layers of pain and rage, but he was still there. She could feel it.

"Lucian," she whispered, her voice trembling with emotion. "Please... I'm so sorry. I didn't mean to hurt you."

Lucian's eyes flickered, just for a moment, but it was enough. Enough for Evelyn to know that he was still fighting, even if he didn't know how.

"You betrayed me," Lucian growled, his voice low and filled with bitterness. "You left me to die, Evelyn. You took everything from me."

Evelyn's heart shattered at his words, but she forced herself to remain steady. "I know," she whispered, her voice thick with sorrow. "I made a terrible mistake. I was weak, and I hurt you. But I'm here now. I'm fighting for you, Lucian. Please... let me help you."

Lucian's jaw clenched, his eyes narrowing as the darkness around him pulsed. "You think you can save me?" he spat, his voice laced with venom. "You think you can undo the damage you've done?"

"I have to try," Evelyn said, her voice stronger now. "I can't leave you like this. I love you, Lucian. I always have."

For a moment, Lucian hesitated. The shadows around him faltered, and she saw a flicker of something in his eyes—something familiar. But then the darkness surged again, wrapping tighter around him, and his expression twisted into one of fury.

"Love?" he snarled, his voice dripping with bitterness. "You don't know the meaning of love. You destroyed me, Evelyn. You broke me. And now there's nothing left."

Evelyn's heart ached, but she didn't back down. "There is something left. I know there is. I saw it, Lucian. You're still in there. I'm not giving up on you. I'll fight for you, even if you can't."

Lucian let out a roar, the sound reverberating through the clearing as the ground beneath them shook. The darkness around him writhed, and he stepped forward, his eyes blazing with fury.

"You think you can fight for me?" he growled. "You think you can undo what's been done? The ancient evil owns me now, Evelyn. I belong to it. And soon, you will too."

Evelyn's breath caught in her throat as Lucian's words hit her like a physical blow. But she didn't retreat. She couldn't. "I won't let that happen," she said, her voice firm. "I'm not giving up on you, Lucian. I love you too much to let the darkness take you."

Lucian's expression twisted in anger, but there was something else beneath it. Fear. Pain. The man he had been was still in there, somewhere, fighting against the ancient evil that had consumed him.

Before Evelyn could say anything else, the ground shook violently, and the shadows around Lucian swirled like a storm, crackling with dark energy. The air was thick with malevolence, and Evelyn knew the final battle had begun.

She took a step forward, her heart pounding in her chest. "Lucian, please," she whispered, her voice breaking. "I'm begging you. Let me save you."

Lucian hesitated, his eyes flickering with something that almost looked like regret. But then the darkness surged again, and he let out a low growl, the pain in his voice unmistakable.

"It's too late," he whispered, his voice filled with sorrow. "It's too late for me."

Evelyn's heart shattered at his words, but she refused to give up. She couldn't. "It's not too late," she said, her voice trembling. "I'll fight for you, Lucian. I'll fight for us."

Lucian's eyes met hers, and for a brief moment, the darkness around him seemed to falter. But then the ground shook again, harder this time, and the air crackled with dark energy as the ancient evil rose to its full power.

The battle had begun, and Evelyn knew it would be the fight of her life.

Chapter 31: "The Carved Shadows"

The forest was unnervingly still as Evelyn, Eldrin, Lila, and Tristan made their way back to the Tree of Sorrows. The air hung heavy with a sense of anticipation, and Evelyn's heart pounded in her chest, knowing that something awaited her at the ancient tree. The fireflies circled overhead, their faint glow casting long shadows across the gnarled roots.

The Tree of Sorrows loomed before them, its bark etched with the scars of those who had come before, leaving behind their pain, their regrets, and their final words. But as Evelyn stepped closer, something drew her in—something new.

"Evelyn?" Lila's voice was cautious, but Evelyn barely heard her. Her eyes were locked on a fresh set of carvings near the base of the tree, the words carved deep into the bark, jagged and raw. Her breath caught in her throat.

Lucian had been here.

Without thinking, Evelyn knelt before the tree, her fingers brushing over the rough, uneven carvings. The words were familiar, hauntingly so. This was Lucian's handwriting—his message, left for her.

With trembling hands, Evelyn traced the lines of the poem he had carved into the tree, and she began to read aloud:

Dark Shadows of My Heart

They rise from the ashes of dreams,

Like serpents coiled in the fog, unseen.

Through the cracks of shattered light, they crawl,

Pulling threads from every wall.

The silence screams between the stars,
A broken moon, a fading scar.
I feel their hands inside my chest,
Tearing out the things I've pressed—
Memories locked in whispered tombs,
Now haunting all my quiet rooms.
Each beat, a thunderous crack,
My heart, a mirror turned to black.
The shadows twist, their edges sharp,
Carving songs of love gone dark.
I scream, but no one hears my cry,
The wind steals breath, the night pulls nigh.
These shadows—my unspoken fears,
Drowning in a sea of tears.
I chase the ghosts who wear my face,
They vanish without a trace,
Leaving me lost in the maze of the night,
No dawn to bring a saving light.
And yet, beneath the wreckage lies
A spark, a flame that never dies.
Through all the shadows tear apart,
I clutch the pieces of my heart.

Tears blurred Evelyn's vision as she finished reading, her voice breaking. Lucian's pain, his sorrow, was laid bare before her, carved into the very heart of the tree. His words were a reflection of the darkness that had consumed him, of the heartbreak he had suffered because of her betrayal. But there, in the final lines, was something more—a spark, a glimmer of hope that had not been entirely extinguished.

"He's still holding on," Evelyn whispered, her fingers brushing over the last lines of the poem. "Despite everything, he hasn't given up completely."

Eldrin stepped closer, his hand resting gently on her shoulder. "This was for you, Evelyn. He left this for you to find."

Her heart ached with the weight of the poem, with the understanding of what Lucian had been through. He had been lost in the darkness, trapped in a sea of shadows and regret. But even through the pain, even through the wreckage of their love, he was still holding on to a part of himself. He hadn't been entirely consumed by the ancient evil.

"I won't give up on him," she said, her voice filled with quiet determination. "He's still in there, and I'm going to bring him back."

Eldrin nodded, his gaze serious. "We need to move quickly. The darkness is growing stronger, and we don't have much time."

Evelyn stood, wiping the tears from her cheeks as she took a final look at the poem. It was a message not only of his despair, but also of his last remaining hope. She couldn't let him slip away—not when he had left her this. Not when there was still a chance to save him.

With her heart heavy but her resolve renewed, she turned to follow the fireflies as they flickered above, their light growing brighter, guiding them deeper into the forest. Lucian was still out there, lost in the shadows, but she would fight to bring him back. She had to.

Chapter 32: "The Weight of Secrets"

The air was thick with tension as the group moved deeper into the forest, the fireflies guiding their way with a soft, flickering light. But there was something different in the atmosphere—a heaviness that hadn't been there before. Evelyn could feel it, and it gnawed at the back of her mind, as if the forest itself was holding its breath.

Eldrin walked slightly ahead, his posture tense, his eyes fixed on the path. Evelyn noticed his silence more acutely now. His usual calm demeanor had been replaced by a quiet intensity, and it worried her. Something was wrong.

"Eldrin," she called softly, quickening her pace to walk beside him. "Are you all right?"

For a moment, he didn't answer, his gaze still locked on the path ahead. But then he stopped, his shoulders sagging as if a great weight had settled on them. His hand reached up, brushing against the carvings on the Tree of Sorrows they had just left behind. His fingers trembled.

"I..." Eldrin's voice cracked, something Evelyn had never heard before. He turned to face her, his eyes glistening with unshed tears. "I didn't expect this."

Evelyn's heart sank as she saw the raw emotion in his eyes. "What is it? What's wrong?"

He took a deep, shuddering breath, his hands dropping to his sides. "The poem... Lucian's poem." His voice wavered. "It brought back... memories."

Eldrin's usual composure shattered as he wiped at his eyes, his face crumbling under the weight of whatever had been hidden beneath the surface for so long. Evelyn had never seen him like this—so vulnerable, so broken.

"I've carried my own shadows," Eldrin said, his voice barely above a whisper. "For years, I've hidden them. But this poem... it felt like a mirror reflecting back everything I've tried to bury."

Evelyn's chest tightened. "What do you mean?"

He turned away, his gaze distant as he stared into the depths of the forest. "Before you, before all of this, I wasn't the man you see now. I... I had my own love. My own heartbreak."

Evelyn's eyes widened in shock. Eldrin had never spoken of his past before, had never shown even a hint of personal sorrow. He had always been strong, unshakable—a guide through the darkness. But now, she realized that he had been hiding his own pain all along.

"She was everything to me," Eldrin continued, his voice hoarse. "But I lost her. And just like Lucian, I was consumed by grief. I wandered this very forest, searching for something—anything—that would take the pain away."

Evelyn's breath caught in her throat. She hadn't known. She hadn't even suspected.

"The darkness in this forest... it almost took me," Eldrin admitted, his voice breaking. "I nearly became what Lucian is now—a man lost to his own shadows."

Evelyn stepped closer, her hand reaching out to touch his arm. "Eldrin... I'm so sorry. I didn't know."

He shook his head, his eyes red with unshed tears. "I never told you because I thought I had moved past it. But when I read Lucian's poem, it all came back—the pain, the loss. His words... they were my words once. My feelings. The same shadows that haunted him once haunted me."

Evelyn's heart ached for him. "But you made it through. You're still here. How?"

Eldrin swallowed hard, his gaze still locked on the darkness beyond the trees. "I fought. I clawed my way back, bit by bit. But it wasn't easy. The forest nearly consumed me. And now, seeing Lucian go through the same thing... I feel like I'm watching myself all over again."

Evelyn squeezed his arm, her voice gentle. "You're not that man anymore, Eldrin. You're stronger now. You've helped me, guided me. You're the reason I still have hope for Lucian."

Eldrin finally looked at her, his expression filled with a mixture of sorrow and gratitude. "I don't know if I'm strong enough to watch someone else fall into the same darkness I almost succumbed to."

Evelyn's grip tightened on his arm. "You're not alone in this. We'll save him—together."

He nodded slowly, his tears falling freely now, a raw display of emotion he had kept locked away for too long. "I believe in you, Evelyn. And I believe in Lucian. But we need to be ready. The darkness we're facing is stronger than anything we've encountered before."

Evelyn nodded, her own emotions swirling inside her. Eldrin's revelation had shaken her, but it also gave her hope. If Eldrin had clawed his way back from the brink of despair, then maybe—just maybe—Lucian could too.

"We'll fight for him," she said softly. "We won't let the darkness win."

The fireflies flickered above them, their light glowing faintly in the heavy air. And for the first time since they had entered the forest, Evelyn felt a small flicker of hope—a belief that, despite the overwhelming odds, they still had a chance.

Chapter 33: "The Gathering Storm"

The forest closed in around them, its gnarled branches twisting into unnatural shapes as the group ventured deeper into its heart. The fireflies flickered dimly, their light barely pushing back the darkness. The air had grown colder, heavier, with each step they took, and Evelyn could feel the weight of the ancient evil pressing down on them, a suffocating presence that made her chest tighten.

Eldrin led the way, his eyes fixed ahead, though his shoulders sagged with the weight of his recent revelation. The pain he carried was fresh, raw, and Evelyn could sense it even though he hadn't spoken a word since they left the Tree of Sorrows. She wanted to comfort him, but she knew there was little comfort to be found here. Not when they were so close to the source of the darkness.

Lila and Tristan walked silently behind them, their faces etched with the same tension that gripped Evelyn's heart. They had all been through so much, and the road ahead was still uncertain. But one thing was clear: the final battle was drawing near.

As they walked, Evelyn's mind kept drifting back to Lucian—his poem, his pain, and the last flicker of hope she had seen in his words. She clung to that hope now, more fiercely than ever, because it was all she had left. If she didn't hold on, she feared she might lose him forever.

"We're getting close," Eldrin said suddenly, his voice low but steady.

Evelyn looked up, her pulse quickening. She could feel it too—the shift in the air, the dark energy that pulsed beneath the ground. They were nearing the heart of the ancient evil. This was the place where everything had started, where the darkness had first taken root. And now, it would be the place where everything ended.

The fireflies slowed, circling a clearing up ahead. The trees parted, revealing a vast, open space that seemed out of place in the dense forest. In the center of the clearing stood a massive, twisted tree—its bark blackened and charred, its branches reaching out like skeletal arms. The air around it buzzed with malevolent energy, and the ground beneath their feet trembled with each step they took.

Evelyn's breath caught in her throat as she stared at the tree. This was it—the source of the ancient evil. The place where the darkness had taken hold of Lucian, twisting his heart into something cold and unforgiving.

Eldrin stopped at the edge of the clearing, his eyes locked on the tree. "This is where it began," he said quietly. "This is where we'll face it."

Evelyn's heart pounded in her chest as she stepped forward, her gaze never leaving the twisted tree. She could feel the darkness here, more intensely than ever before. It seeped into her bones, into her very soul, and she knew that the battle ahead would be unlike anything they had faced before.

Lila moved closer to Evelyn, her voice tense. "What's the plan?"

Evelyn swallowed hard, her mind racing. She didn't have all the answers, but she knew one thing: they couldn't fight the darkness alone. They needed Lucian.

"We need to get to Lucian," Evelyn said, her voice firm despite the fear that clawed at her insides. "He's the key to this. If we can reach him, if we can pull him back from the darkness, we'll have a chance."

"And if we can't?" Tristan asked, his voice grim.

Evelyn's heart clenched at the thought, but she pushed it aside. She couldn't think like that. She wouldn't let herself.

"We will," she said, her voice steely. "We have to."

The group moved cautiously into the clearing, their footsteps soft on the trembling earth. As they neared the twisted tree, the air grew colder, and the shadows around them thickened, twisting and writhing like living things.

Suddenly, the ground beneath them shook violently, and a deep, guttural roar echoed through the clearing. The air crackled with dark energy, and from the shadows, a figure emerged—wreathed in darkness, his form barely recognizable beneath the writhing shadows that clung to him like a second skin.

Lucian.

Evelyn's breath caught in her throat as she saw him, her heart breaking all over again. He was there, but he wasn't the Lucian she had known. The ancient evil had taken him, twisted him into something dark, something almost monstrous. His eyes glowed with a cold, red light, and the shadows around him pulsed with malevolent energy.

But beneath it all, Evelyn could still see him. The man she loved was still there, somewhere deep inside the darkness.

"Lucian," she whispered, her voice trembling. "Please, don't do this."

Lucian's eyes flickered, but the darkness around him surged, wrapping tighter around his body. He let out a low growl, his voice barely human. "It's too late, Evelyn. There's nothing left."

Evelyn's heart shattered at his words, but she refused to give up. She stepped forward, her hand outstretched, her voice filled with desperation. "No, it's not too late. I know you're still in there. I know you can fight this."

The ground shook again, and the shadows writhed around Lucian, as if they were alive, feeding off his pain, his anger. He took a step toward her, his movements slow and deliberate, the darkness clinging to him like a weight.

"You can't save me," he growled, his voice thick with sorrow. "You couldn't before, and you can't now."

Evelyn's heart clenched, but she kept her gaze steady, her voice firm. "I'm not giving up on you. I love you, Lucian. I always have. And I'll fight for you until the end."

The air crackled with tension as Lucian's eyes met hers, a flicker of something familiar passing through the cold, red glow. For a moment, the shadows around him seemed to hesitate, as if the ancient evil was losing its grip.

But then the ground shook violently, and the darkness surged again, stronger this time, pulling Lucian further into its grasp.

"We have to stop it!" Eldrin shouted, his voice filled with urgency.

Evelyn's heart raced as she looked at Lucian, her mind spinning with fear and desperation. The darkness was too strong. They couldn't fight it alone.

But they weren't alone.

The fireflies circled above, their light growing brighter, and Evelyn felt a surge of hope. The magic of the forest wasn't gone. There was still a chance.

"We need the fireflies!" Evelyn shouted, her voice filled with determination. "They'll help us!"

The fireflies descended, their light growing brighter and brighter until it was almost blinding. The shadows recoiled, and for the first time, Evelyn saw Lucian clearly. He was weak, his body trembling beneath the weight of the darkness, but he was still there. He was still fighting.

"Lucian," Evelyn whispered, stepping closer. "Please. Come back to me."

The fireflies swarmed around him, their light pushing back the darkness, and for a moment, everything seemed to still. Evelyn held her breath, her heart pounding in her chest, waiting—hoping—for Lucian to break free.

And then, slowly, his eyes softened. The cold, red glow faded, and she saw him—the real Lucian—looking back at her, his eyes filled with pain, but also with love.

"Evelyn..." he whispered, his voice barely audible.

Evelyn's heart leaped as she rushed forward, her hands reaching for his. "Lucian, I'm here. I'm not leaving you."

But before she could reach him, the shadows surged again, pulling him back into the darkness.

The final battle had begun.

Chapter 34: "Tree of Mirrors"

The path to the Tree of Mirrors was suffocatingly silent. The fireflies barely lit the way now, their faint glow swallowed by the thickening fog. Evelyn's heart raced as the tree loomed ahead, its bark shimmering like glass, reflecting the twisted shadows around it. A cold chill settled over her, far more than just the night air. There was something ancient about this place, something wrong.

Eldrin slowed, his hand raised as if to halt their advance. "The Tree of Mirrors," he murmured, his voice low and tense. "It reveals more than just reflections. It shows the soul."

The words settled heavily over them as they approached the massive tree. Its bark was smooth, too smooth, like a mirror made of ice. Branches twisted upward, the leaves rustling softly though no wind blew. The air itself felt alive, thick with unseen eyes watching their every move.

Evelyn stepped forward cautiously, her pulse hammering in her ears. The closer she got, the more distorted the world around her became. Her reflection began to form on the shimmering surface, but it wasn't hers.

Instead of her own face, Lucian's stared back at her. But not the Lucian she had once known—his eyes were hollow, shadows clung to his face, and his expression was twisted with pain. Evelyn's heart clenched as she stepped closer, drawn to the ghostly image of him.

"Lucian," she whispered, reaching out to touch the bark.

The surface of the tree rippled under her fingers like water, the image of Lucian wavering but not disappearing. His eyes locked onto hers, cold and empty, but beneath that was something she could almost reach—his sorrow, his love, buried beneath the layers of darkness.

"You left me," the reflection whispered, Lucian's voice low and broken, sending a shiver down her spine. "You betrayed me."

Evelyn recoiled, her hand trembling as the words cut through her. "No... I didn't mean to," she whispered, but the reflection did not respond. The image of Lucian remained, hollow, ghostly, a twisted mirror of the man she loved. Her breath caught in her throat, and she stepped back, the cold settling deep into her bones.

Behind her, Lila approached the tree cautiously, her eyes wide. As she drew near, her reflection began to form in the smooth bark, but just like Evelyn, it wasn't her own face she saw.

It was the face of her younger brother, lost to the darkness years ago. His wide, innocent eyes stared back at her, but his mouth twisted into a sad smile.

"Why didn't you save me?" the reflection asked, the voice barely a whisper.

Lila's breath caught. "I tried," she whispered, tears welling in her eyes. "I tried so hard."

The reflection of her brother's face contorted, darkening, as if being pulled into the shadows. "You left me behind," he said softly, his voice echoing with a hollow emptiness. "I was alone."

Lila fell to her knees, her face crumpling in sorrow. "I'm so sorry," she sobbed, reaching out toward the image, but like Evelyn, her hand passed through the bark as though it were nothing but mist.

Tristan, who had been watching silently, took an unsteady step toward the tree, drawn in despite his better judgment. The surface shimmered, and his reflection began to form. It was a man—stern, towering, and hard-eyed. His father. The man who had walked out on him when he was just a child.

Tristan's mouth twisted in anger, but his eyes betrayed his pain. "You," he hissed, stepping closer to the image. "You left me."

The reflection of his father stared back at him, emotionless, cold, unmoving. "You were weak," the reflection said, the voice deep and haunting. "You were always weak."

Tristan's fists clenched at his sides, his jaw tightening. "I survived without you," he growled, though his voice trembled. "I didn't need you."

The image didn't waver, the man's face hard and distant. "You've never been enough," the reflection said, the words hanging in the air like a death sentence.

Tristan let out a sharp breath, his eyes burning, but he couldn't move. The tree held him in place, the reflection searing into him, opening old wounds that had never fully healed.

Eldrin stood off to the side, silent, but Evelyn saw the tension in his posture, the way his shoulders sagged. He stepped forward at last, almost against his will, and the tree's surface rippled to meet him. His reflection came slowly, like a nightmare rising from the depths.

It was a woman—beautiful, ethereal, but her face was etched with sorrow. Her eyes, once filled with light, now only reflected grief. The image of her pulled at something deep inside Eldrin, and for the first time, Evelyn saw the cracks in his unshakable exterior.

"I failed you," he whispered, his voice hoarse.

The reflection said nothing, but the sadness in her eyes spoke volumes. Eldrin stood frozen, the weight of the past pressing down on him like a crushing tide. He had buried this pain deep, but the tree had ripped It to the surface, and now there was no escaping it.

"I couldn't save you," Eldrin whispered, tears slipping down his face. "I couldn't stop it."

The image of the woman shimmered, her eyes filling with tears before she slowly faded, leaving only the cold surface of the tree behind. Eldrin dropped to his knees, his breath ragged, his hands shaking.

The silence that followed was thick, heavy with the weight of everything the Tree of Mirrors had revealed. Their ghosts, their deepest fears, had been laid bare before them, and each of them carried the burden of that revelation.

Evelyn's heart pounded in her chest, her pulse racing. The reflection of Lucian still lingered in her mind, his words echoing over and over. You betrayed me.

They couldn't stay here. The longer they stood before the tree, the more it dug its roots into their souls, trapping them in a cycle of regret and pain. But how could they move forward with the weight of their pasts still clinging to them?

"We have to leave," Eldrin rasped, his voice raw. He pushed himself to his feet, his face pale and drawn. "The tree... it will trap us here. We can't let it."

Evelyn nodded, but her legs felt heavy, as though the tree had tethered her in place. Slowly, she tore her gaze away from the shimmering surface, stepping back into the fog that swirled around the clearing.

The fireflies circled above, their dim light barely piercing the thick atmosphere of the forest. As they moved away from the tree, Evelyn felt the cold begin to lift, but the images it had shown them lingered, ghosts that would not easily be forgotten.

Chapter 35: "The Gathering Shadows"

The fireflies' glow barely cut through the thick fog as Evelyn, Eldrin, Lila, and Tristan moved away from the Tree of Mirrors. The reflections they had seen still clung to their minds like ghosts, their faces pale and drawn as the weight of the past pressed down on them. The eerie quiet of the forest wrapped around them, the oppressive silence broken only by the sound of their own footsteps.

Evelyn's heart still raced, her thoughts consumed by the image of Lucian that had stared back at her from the tree's mirrored surface. You betrayed me. The words echoed in her mind, twisting her stomach into knots. She couldn't escape the weight of it, even as she tried to focus on the path ahead.

Eldrin led the group, his face tense and pale. The sorrow and regret he carried were heavy in the air, but he kept moving, his determination clear. Whatever the ancient evil had in store for them, they couldn't let the Tree of Mirrors trap them in their pain. Not now.

Lila was quiet, her eyes downcast as they walked. The image of her brother—his haunting, broken voice—lingered over her like a dark cloud. Tristan kept his distance, his face hard but his eyes reflecting the turmoil beneath the surface. His father's words had cut him deeper than he would ever admit.

The silence between them was suffocating, but none of them dared to break it. The forest itself seemed to grow darker, the shadows deeper, and the path ahead twisted and turned, as if the forest were alive, shifting with every step they took. The ancient evil was close. They could feel it.

After what felt like hours, Eldrin finally spoke, his voice barely above a whisper. "We're nearing the heart of the darkness. The place where the ancient evil is strongest."

Evelyn's breath caught in her throat. The air here was heavier, darker, as if the very ground beneath their feet pulsed with malevolent energy. The fireflies flickered erratically, their light dimming as if they, too, were afraid of what lay ahead.

"We have to keep going," Evelyn said, her voice shaky but firm. "We're so close."

Eldrin nodded, but his eyes were distant, his thoughts clearly still entangled with what he had seen at the Tree of Mirrors. "Be ready," he murmured. "The forest will try to stop us. It feeds off our fears, our pain. Don't let it."

They continued forward, their steps cautious as they moved through the thickening fog. The trees seemed to close in around them, their twisted branches reaching out like skeletal fingers. The air grew colder with each step, and the weight of the ancient evil pressed down on them like a suffocating blanket.

Suddenly, the ground beneath them trembled. Evelyn's heart leaped into her throat as the earth shifted, and a deep, rumbling growl echoed through the forest. The shadows around them pulsed, alive with dark energy, and from the mist emerged a figure—towering and monstrous, its form barely visible through the swirling fog.

Eldrin drew his weapon, his eyes narrowing. "It's here."

The creature moved slowly toward them, its massive form cloaked in shadows, its eyes glowing with an unnatural light. Evelyn's pulse quickened as she took a step back, her hand tightening around the hilt of her blade. The ancient evil wasn't going to let them get any closer—not without a fight.

"Stay together," Eldrin commanded, his voice steady despite the fear that hung thick in the air. "We can't let it separate us."

The creature let out another deep growl, the sound reverberating through the forest, shaking the very ground beneath their feet. Evelyn's heart raced as she tried to steady her breathing, her thoughts spinning. They had come so far, fought so hard. They couldn't fail now.

The fireflies circled around them, their light flickering wildly as if trying to push back the shadows. But the darkness was too strong, too powerful. The creature lunged forward, its massive claws tearing through the fog, aiming for Eldrin.

He moved swiftly, his sword flashing in the dim light as he deflected the attack. But the creature was relentless, its movements fluid and deadly as it closed in on them.

Evelyn's heart pounded in her chest as she charged forward, her blade slicing through the air. She struck at the creature's side, but it barely reacted, its massive form absorbing the blow as if it were nothing more than a whisper.

"We can't fight it like this!" Lila shouted, her voice laced with panic.

Eldrin grimaced, his eyes never leaving the creature. "We need to weaken it. The fireflies—they'll help us."

The fireflies swarmed around the creature, their light growing brighter, more intense. The shadows around the creature recoiled slightly, but the ancient evil was too strong. It let out a deafening roar, its glowing eyes locking onto Evelyn.

Her heart froze as the creature lunged toward her, its massive claws outstretched. She barely had time to move, but before the blow could land, a blast of light erupted from the fireflies, blinding the creature and forcing it back.

Eldrin stepped forward, his voice filled with urgency. "Now! While it's weak!"

Evelyn's pulse raced as she moved forward, her blade gleaming in the light of the fireflies. With a surge of adrenaline, she plunged her sword into the creature's side, the force of the blow sending it staggering back.

The creature let out a bloodcurdling roar, its body convulsing as the fireflies swarmed around it, their light growing brighter and brighter, pushing back the darkness.

For a moment, everything was still. The creature stood frozen, its glowing eyes wide with rage. And then, with one final, ear-splitting scream, it collapsed to the ground, its body dissolving into a cloud of shadows that melted into the earth.

The air was thick with silence, the only sound the soft buzzing of the fireflies as they circled overhead.

Evelyn's breath came in ragged gasps as she stepped back, her heart pounding. They had won—for now. But the battle was far from over. The ancient evil was still out there, lurking in the shadows, waiting for its chance to strike.

"We need to keep moving," Eldrin said quietly, his voice tense. "This isn't over."

Evelyn nodded, her heart heavy with the weight of what was still to come. The fireflies flickered above them, their light dimming once more as they began to lead the way forward.

The final battle was drawing near, and Evelyn knew that the worst was yet to come.

Chapter 36: "Echoes of the Fallen"

The fireflies' light continued to guide them through the dense fog, their glow dim and flickering as if the forest itself was trying to swallow their light. Evelyn, Eldrin, Lila, and Tristan trudged forward, their breaths visible in the frigid air. The battle had left them exhausted, their bodies heavy, and their spirits weighed down by the knowledge that the ancient evil still lurked, biding its time.

Evelyn's hand trembled as she gripped her blade, the image of the monstrous creature still fresh in her mind. She could feel the ancient evil watching them, whispering in the wind that rustled the leaves. Every step felt like a descent into a deeper darkness, the forest closing in around them like a cage.

Eldrin moved ahead, his eyes fixed on the path. His expression was one of grim determination, but there was a flicker of doubt in his eyes that Evelyn hadn't seen before. The Tree of Mirrors had revealed truths that had left scars on all of them, and she could see the weight of it pressing down on him. She wanted to say something, to offer a word of comfort, but the words caught in her throat. What comfort could she give when her own heart felt as heavy as stone?

Tristan kept his hand on Lila's shoulder, the only sign of reassurance he could offer as they walked through the gloom. Lila's face was pale, her eyes haunted by the vision of her brother. She had not spoken a word since they left the Tree of Mirrors, her silence a shroud over the group. The only sound was the crunch of dead leaves beneath their boots and the distant howl of the wind.

Eldrin finally stopped, raising his hand to signal the group. "We're close," he whispered, his voice barely audible above the rustling trees. "The source of the ancient evil is near. We must be prepared for anything."

The fireflies hovered In front of them, their light forming a trail through the dense undergrowth. Evelyn felt her heart race as she looked ahead. The trees seemed to part, revealing a path that led down into a deep, shadowed valley. The air was colder here, biting at her skin, and a sense of foreboding settled over her.

Evelyn swallowed hard. "What's down there?" she asked, her voice unsteady.

Eldrin's face was grim. "A place where the fallen dwell. Spirits trapped by the ancient evil's power. We must tread carefully. Their pain fuels the darkness."

As they descended into the valley, the temperature dropped even further. The fog thickened, wrapping around them like tendrils of smoke. Shadows moved along the periphery of their vision, whispering words that clawed at their minds. Evelyn could barely make out the words, but they were filled with sorrow, regret, and anger. It was as if the very souls of the dead cried out for release.

Lila shivered, clutching her arms. "I can hear them," she whispered, her voice barely a breath. "They're suffering."

Evelyn reached for her hand, squeezing it gently. "We'll get through this. We have to."

Tristan scanned their surroundings, his eyes narrowed. "This place feels wrong. It's like it's alive, and it's watching us."

Eldrin nodded, his grip tightening on his weapon. "Stay close. If we get separated, the forest will consume us."

They continued deeper into the valley, and the path grew narrower, the trees twisting into grotesque shapes. Evelyn's skin prickled as she sensed the presence of the fallen spirits all around them. The whispers grew louder, filling her head with images of broken hearts, lost love, and betrayal. She felt her own guilt rising, the memory of Lucian's eyes staring at her from the Tree of Mirrors.

A sudden cry pierced the air—a wail so full of pain and despair that it sent a shiver down Evelyn's spine. The fireflies scattered, their light flickering as the shadows around them thickened, forming shapes that moved with unnatural speed. Out of the darkness, figures emerged—spectral and translucent, their faces contorted in agony.

Evelyn gasped as she recognized the first figure. It was Lucian, his eyes hollow, his face twisted in grief. "You left me," he whispered, his voice echoing like a cold wind through the valley. "You betrayed me."

Evelyn felt her heart twist. "I'm sorry," she breathed, her eyes stinging with tears. "I didn't mean to—"

The shadowy form of Lucian reached out, his hand passing through her as a chill settled over her heart. "Your words mean nothing now. You can't undo what's been done."

Before she could respond, more figures emerged from the mist—specters of those the ancient evil had claimed. Each one carried their own sorrow, their own pain, and their eyes bore Into the group with a hunger that spoke of years spent in torment.

Lila stepped back, her face pale. "What do they want?"

Eldrin's voice was grim. "They want release. But the ancient evil has bound them here, feeding off their anguish. We must not let them touch us, or we will be lost to the darkness."

The spirits closed in, their hands reaching out, their eyes full of longing and rage. Evelyn's breath quickened as she raised her blade, ready to defend herself. The fireflies' light flickered, struggling to keep the shadows at bay.

Tristan swung his weapon, his movements precise as he struck at the approaching spirits. "We have to keep moving!"

The spirits hissed, their forms dissolving into mist as they recoiled from the blows. But for every one they repelled, two more took its place, their wails filling the air with a sound that sent chills down Evelyn's spine.

Eldrin pushed forward, cutting a path through the spirits. "Follow me! We have to reach the altar—the source of their torment."

Evelyn, Lila, and Tristan followed closely behind, their weapons slashing through the ghostly forms that tried to drag them down. The valley seemed to stretch on forever, the shadows growing thicker with each step. The air was heavy, and Evelyn could feel the ancient evil's power increasing, the malevolent energy clawing at her.

After what felt like an eternity, they reached a clearing. At its center stood an ancient stone altar, covered in runes that glowed faintly in the fireflies' light. The ground around it was littered with bones and tattered remnants of those who had fallen victim to the ancient evil.

Eldrin stopped, his eyes locked on the altar. "This is it. We must destroy it."

Evelyn felt a surge of determination. "How?"

"The runes," Eldrin said. "They bind the spirits. We need to break them."

As the group moved toward the altar, the shadows around them thickened, forming a swirling mass of darkness. The spirits cried out, their voices filled with desperation. Evelyn's heart pounded as she raised her blade, slashing at the shadows that tried to pull her back.

Eldrin knelt by the altar, tracing his fingers over the runes. "It's a binding spell, ancient and powerful. I need time to break it."

Lila and Tristan formed a protective circle around him, their weapons flashing as they fended off the spirits that surged toward them. Evelyn fought beside them, her movements swift as she struck at the shadows.

"Almost there!" Eldrin shouted, his hands glowing as he chanted the incantation to break the spell.

The fireflies' light intensified, casting the clearing in a bright glow. The shadows recoiled, their wails turning to screams of anger as the runes began to crack and shatter. The ground beneath them trembled, and the spirits surrounding them let out a final, anguished cry before dissolving into the mist.

With a surge of energy, Eldrin slammed his hand down on the altar. The runes shattered, and a wave of light burst forth, pushing the darkness back. The spirits vanished, their cries fading into silence as the power of the ancient evil weakened.

Evelyn felt the air grow lighter, the oppressive weight lifting as the altar's power broke. The fireflies hovered around them, their light calm and steady once more.

Eldrin stood, his face pale but relieved. "We've weakened its hold, but the ancient evil is still out there. This was only one of its many strongholds."

Evelyn nodded, her grip on her blade tightening. "We'll find the others. We'll end this."

As they moved out of the valley, the fireflies led the way, their glow a beacon of hope against the darkness that still lingered. The battle was far from over, but Evelyn felt a spark of determination in her chest.

They would fight, and they would win. The ancient evil would not claim their souls.

Not today.

Chapter 38: "The Veil of Darkness"

The fireflies led the way, their light carving a narrow path through the twisted trees and thickening fog. The group moved cautiously, their senses heightened, each of them attuned to the forest's unsettling silence. The air felt heavier, the shadows seemed to deepen with every step, and Evelyn couldn't shake the feeling that they were being watched.

Eldrin kept his pace steady, his eyes constantly scanning the darkness. Lila and Tristan remained close behind, their faces tight with concentration. Evelyn walked beside them, her hand resting on the hilt of her blade. She could feel the forest pressing in on them, whispering threats and promises of despair.

The silence between them was thick, and though they all felt the weight of the journey, there was a sense of purpose holding them together. They had faced the cursed spirits, broken one of the ancient evil's strongholds, and each of them knew that this was only the beginning. The deeper they ventured, the stronger the darkness became, feeding off their fears and their pasts.

The path twisted, leading them to a ravine filled with thorny vines and dead trees. The ground was covered in a thick layer of fog, and the air was colder here, biting into their skin. Evelyn felt a shiver run down her spine. "Is this the right way?" she asked, her voice barely above a whisper.

Eldrin nodded, his expression grim. "Yes. The fireflies have brought us here for a reason. We're getting close."

Tristan frowned, his eyes scanning the shadows. "It feels like a trap."

Eldrin's grip on his weapon tightened. "It is. The ancient evil will do everything it can to stop us. But we have no choice. We have to push forward."

Evelyn's gaze moved to the ravine ahead. It was shrouded in darkness, the kind that seemed to swallow the light. The fireflies' glow dimmed as they hovered above it, their light barely illuminating the twisted vines below. "We need to be careful," she said, her voice steady. "This place feels... wrong."

Lila shivered. "It's like the air itself is heavy with hate."

Evelyn nodded, her hand tightening on her blade. "Stay close. Don't let anything separate us."

As they made their way down the ravine, the air grew colder, and the whispers became louder. The shadows shifted, taking on shapes that moved and slithered between the vines. Evelyn could feel the presence of the ancient evil, its power radiating through the darkness. Her heart pounded in her chest, and she forced herself to keep moving, knowing that they couldn't turn back now.

Suddenly, a sharp cry echoed through the air, and the ground beneath their feet trembled. Evelyn's heart leaped into her throat as the shadows surged forward, wrapping around the vines and forming figures that reached out with claw-like hands.

"Get ready!" Eldrin shouted, raising his weapon.

The shadows lunged, their forms twisting and shifting as they charged at the group. Evelyn drew her blade, her movements swift as she sliced through the darkness. The fireflies circled above, their light flickering as they tried to push back the shadows.

Tristan and Lila fought beside her, their weapons flashing as they struck at the spectral figures. The air was filled with the sounds of battle—clashing steel, the hiss of shadows recoiling, and the cries of the ancient evil that seemed to seep from every corner of the ravine.

Eldrin's voice rose above the chaos. "The fireflies are weakening—stay close! We have to get through this!"

Evelyn's breath came in ragged gasps as she fought, her blade cutting through the shadows that swarmed around her. The darkness felt alive, each strike she made barely enough to keep it at bay. She glanced over at Lila, who was struggling against a shadowy figure that had wrapped its tendrils around her arm.

"Lila!" Evelyn shouted, rushing to her side.

With a swift strike, she severed the tendrils, pulling Lila back just as another shadow lunged toward them. The two fought side by side, their blades flashing as they defended themselves against the onslaught.

Eldrin moved ahead, his weapon a blur as he cut through the shadows that blocked their path. "We need to find the source of the darkness—it's coming from deeper within the ravine!"

The group pressed on, their movements coordinated as they fought their way through the shadows. The fireflies' light flickered weakly, their glow dimming as the darkness grew thicker. Evelyn could feel the ancient evil's power intensifying, a cold, suffocating presence that pressed down on them like a weight.

As they moved further into the ravine, the shadows became more aggressive, their attacks relentless. Evelyn's muscles ached, and her breath came In sharp bursts as she struggled to keep up the fight. She could see the exhaustion in Lila's eyes, the strain in Tristan's movements, but they all pushed forward, driven by a shared determination.

At the end of the ravine, a faint light flickered in the distance. Evelyn's heart quickened. "There—do you see it?"

Eldrin nodded, his eyes locked on the light. "That's it. The source of the veil. If we reach it, we might be able to dispel the darkness."

The group surged forward, their pace quickening as they fought through the last wave of shadows. The fireflies circled around them, their light merging with the distant glow as they moved closer. Evelyn's pulse raced as she saw what lay ahead—a massive stone archway, similar to the one they had encountered before, but this one was covered in vines and thorns.

The archway pulsed with dark energy, the runes etched into its surface glowing with an unnatural light. The air around it was thick with malevolent power, and Evelyn could feel the ancient evil's presence radiating from it.

Eldrin raised his hand, signaling for the group to stop. "This is it—the heart of the darkness in this part of the forest. We need to destroy it."

Tristan's eyes were hard as he gripped his weapon. "How?"

Eldrin pulled out another vial of the purifying elixir. "The runes are the key. We break them, and the darkness will fade."

Evelyn's grip tightened on her blade. "Let's do it."

As Eldrin approached the archway, the shadows around them surged, forming a wall that blocked their path. The fireflies' light dimmed, struggling against the wave of darkness that threatened to overwhelm them.

"Protect him!" Evelyn shouted, charging forward with Lila and Tristan. They formed a defensive circle around Eldrin, their weapons flashing as they struck at the shadows. The air was filled with the hissing cries of the ancient evil, its voice echoing in their minds.

Eldrin poured the elixir over the runes, his hands glowing as he chanted the incantation. The shadows recoiled, and the archway trembled, cracks forming along its surface as the runes began to fade.

Evelyn fought with everything she had, her movements quick and precise as she kept the shadows at bay. Lila and Tristan moved with her, their blades slicing through the darkness as they held their ground.

The archway shuddered, the runes cracking as light spilled out from the fissures. The fireflies' glow intensified, merging with the light as it pushed back the shadows.

"Almost there!" Eldrin shouted, his voice filled with urgency.

Evelyn's breath came in gasps as she struck at the last wave of shadows. "We've got this!"

With a final surge of energy, Eldrin slammed his hand down on the archway. The runes shattered, and a burst of light exploded from the stone, pushing the darkness back. The shadows screamed as they dissolved into mist, their forms vanishing as the light filled the ravine.

The air grew warm, and the oppressive weight lifted as the fireflies' light filled the space, their glow calm and steady once more. The ancient evil's hold on the ravine had been broken.

Evelyn lowered her blade, her breath ragged but relieved. They had succeeded. Another piece of the ancient evil's power had been weakened.

Eldrin turned to the group, his expression resolute. "This is only the beginning. The final battle draws near, and we must be prepared."

Evelyn nodded, her eyes fixed on the path ahead. "We'll keep moving. We'll find every last stronghold and destroy them."

As they continued through the forest, the fireflies led the way, their light a beacon against the darkness. Evelyn felt the determination burn within her. They were getting closer to ending this, and no matter what lay ahead, she was ready.

The shadows would not have the last word.

Chapter 39: "The Whispering Abyss"

The fireflies' light illuminated the path ahead, a narrow trail that led deeper into the forest's heart. The air grew colder, and the shadows twisted like claws, reaching for Evelyn, Eldrin, Lila, and Tristan as they pressed onward. The forest's whispering voices seemed louder here, an unending murmur that gnawed at the edges of Evelyn's mind. It was as if the forest itself was alive, a living, breathing entity determined to devour them whole.

Evelyn's fingers brushed against the pendant around her neck—a gift from her mother long ago. It had always brought her comfort, a reminder of a time when she believed in light and hope. Now, with the darkness pressing in around them, she clung to it as if it were the only thing keeping her grounded.

"Stay close," Eldrin warned, his voice low and tense. "The next stronghold isn't far, but it's guarded. The ancient evil won't let us reach it easily."

Lila's face was pale, her eyes darting around as the shadows whispered to her, calling her name. "It feels like... like the forest knows us, like it's alive."

Tristan nodded, his grip on his weapon tightening. "It is. And it's trying to break us."

Evelyn swallowed, forcing down the fear that clawed at her throat. "We won't let it." She could feel the determination burning within her, a flame that refused to die despite the overwhelming darkness.

As they continued, the path narrowed, the trees closing in until their branches tangled overhead, blocking out the sky. The fog thickened, and the whispers grew louder, transforming into a chorus of voices—some pleading, others filled with rage. Evelyn felt her skin prickle as she recognized one of the voices. It was Lucian, his voice a distant echo. Why did you leave me?

Evelyn's heart clenched, but she forced herself to move forward. The forest was playing tricks, trying to drag her into the past. She couldn't let it. She glanced at Eldrin, who was scanning the path ahead with a grim expression.

After what felt like hours of walking through the oppressive fog, they reached a vast chasm—the Whispering Abyss. The ground dropped off into darkness, the edges lined with jagged rocks that jutted out like fangs. The air was colder here, and the whispers were no longer just voices; they had become screams, filled with pain and despair.

Eldrin paused at the edge of the abyss, his eyes narrowed as he studied the darkness below. "The stronghold is on the other side. But we'll need to cross carefully."

Lila shivered, her hand clutching her pendant. "How? There's no bridge."

Eldrin reached into his bag, pulling out a small crystal that glowed with a soft blue light. "This is a binding stone. It can create a temporary bridge, but it will only last for a short time. We need to move fast."

Tristan looked down into the chasm, his face tense. "And if we fall?"

Eldrin's expression was grim. "If you fall, you're lost to the whispers. The abyss will consume you."

Evelyn felt a shiver run down her spine. The abyss seemed to pulse with a malevolent energy, and the whispers clawed at her mind, filling her with doubts. She took a deep breath, trying to steady herself. "Let's do it. We don't have a choice."

Eldrin nodded, holding the crystal over the edge of the chasm. He whispered an incantation, and the stone flared with light. The ground beneath them trembled, and a narrow bridge of light began to form, stretching across the abyss. It glowed with a pale, ethereal light, flickering as if struggling to hold its shape.

"Go!" Eldrin commanded, his voice urgent. "Move quickly!"

Evelyn was the first to step onto the bridge. The moment her foot touched the light, a cold shock ran through her body, and the whispers intensified, screaming in her ears. You will fail. You cannot win.

She gritted her teeth, forcing herself to take another step. The bridge wavered beneath her feet, but she pushed forward, her gaze fixed on the far side of the chasm.

Lila and Tristan followed, their steps careful and measured. The light beneath them flickered, and the abyss seemed to reach up, shadowy tendrils clawing at their legs as they moved. Evelyn's heart pounded as she heard Lila gasp, nearly losing her balance.

"Hold on!" Evelyn shouted, reaching out to steady her. "We're almost there."

Lila nodded, her face pale as she regained her footing. The bridge continued to shake, the light dimming as the whispers grew louder, almost deafening. The forest was trying to tear them apart.

Eldrin was the last to step onto the bridge, his eyes locked on the far side. "Keep moving! The crystal's power won't last much longer."

Evelyn quickened her pace, the far side of the abyss drawing closer. She could feel the ancient evil's power pressing against them, trying to push them off balance. The fireflies swarmed around, their light struggling to fend off the darkness that surged from below.

Just as they reached the halfway point, the bridge shuddered violently, and a massive shadow rose from the depths of the chasm—a figure with eyes like burning coals, its form wreathed in smoke and darkness. It let out a roar that shook the air, and its clawed hands reached for them, ripping at the bridge.

Evelyn's pulse raced as she dodged the creature's attack, her blade flashing as she struck at its claw. The bridge wavered, and the light flickered, but she held her ground, fighting to keep her balance.

Tristan swung his weapon, striking the shadow as it lunged for Lila. "Stay close!"

Eldrin's voice rose above the chaos. "We have to get to the other side—now!"

The group surged forward, their pace quickening as the creature clawed at the bridge. Evelyn's breath came in gasps as she fought her way across, her eyes fixed on the far side. The light beneath them flickered one last time, and she felt the bridge beginning to dissolve.

With a final burst of speed, they reached the other side, just as the bridge shattered into fragments of light. The creature's roar echoed through the abyss as the ground beneath them solidified, and the whispers faded into silence.

Evelyn collapsed onto her knees, her heart pounding as she caught her breath. They had made it, but the fight had drained her. She looked up to see Eldrin standing at the edge, his expression grim.

"We've crossed the Whispering Abyss, but the stronghold is just ahead." He pointed to a massive stone door covered in runes. "That's the entrance."

Evelyn forced herself to stand, her gaze fixed on the door. "What's behind it?"

Eldrin's eyes were dark. "The ancient evil's lair. One of the strongest we've faced yet. It will be waiting for us."

Tristan nodded, his face set with determination. "Then we fight."

Lila's hand tightened around her pendant. "Whatever it takes, we end this."

Evelyn felt the fire inside her ignite once more. "We've come this far. We won't back down now."

As the group approached the stone door, the fireflies gathered around them, their light forming a protective barrier. Evelyn's heart raced as she prepared for what lay ahead. This battle would be unlike any they had faced before, but she was ready.

The ancient evil had taken too much from them. It was time to fight back, and this time, they would not let the darkness win.

Chapter 40: "The Heart of the Forest"

The fireflies glowed brighter as the group moved through the dense thicket. Each step felt heavier than the last, the forest pressing in as if it knew their Intentions. The air was thick with tension, the silence broken only by the rustle of leaves and the distant echoes of whispers. Evelyn's pulse quickened as they approached the entrance to the ancient evil's final stronghold—The Heart of the Forest.

The path wound like a serpent, twisting through gnarled trees and under hanging vines. The ground was littered with fallen leaves that seemed to whisper underfoot, and the shadows loomed, forming shapes that twisted and writhed in the dim light. Evelyn's hand rested on her blade, every sense heightened as the forest pulsed with malevolent energy.

Eldrin moved ahead, his eyes locked on the path. He carried the crystal they had used to cross the Whispering Abyss, but its light was fading, as if the forest was draining its power. "We're close," he said, his voice a whisper that blended with the sighing wind. "The Heart of the Forest lies ahead. Prepare yourselves."

Lila's eyes darted around, and she clutched her pendant tightly. "It's as if the forest knows what we're about to do."

Tristan nodded, his face set with determination. "It's afraid. It knows we've come to end its reign."

Evelyn glanced at Eldrin, seeing the tension in his eyes. He had grown quieter since crossing the Whispering Abyss, his expression a mask of grim resolve. She wanted to ask him what was on his mind, but the weight of the moment pressed down on her, and she focused on the path ahead.

They reached a massive clearing where the trees formed a circle, their twisted branches intertwining like skeletal fingers. At the center of the clearing stood a giant tree—The Heart of the Forest. Its bark was blackened, covered in pulsating runes that glowed with a sickly green light. The air around it was heavy, the ground pulsing as if alive, and the shadows cast by the tree seemed to stretch and shift, clawing at the edges of the clearing.

Eldrin raised his hand, signaling the group to stop. "This is it. The source of the ancient evil."

Evelyn's breath caught in her throat as she stared at the tree. It was massive, its twisted roots spreading out like veins, and she could feel the darkness emanating from it. It was as if the tree itself was the beating heart of the evil that had consumed the forest. "How do we destroy it?" she asked, her voice a mix of determination and fear.

Eldrin's eyes darkened. "We need to break the runes. They bind the ancient evil to the forest, feeding off the pain and sorrow trapped here."

Tristan moved to Evelyn's side, his weapon drawn. "And the moment we start, it's going to fight back."

Eldrin nodded, pulling out the vial of purifying elixir. "Once we pour this over the runes, it will weaken the tree's hold, but it won't be enough. We'll need to strike at the heart, the center of the runes. But know this—when we do, the forest will react violently. We must be prepared for anything."

Lila's hand tightened on her weapon. "We're ready."

As Eldrin approached the tree, the shadows shifted, and the ground trembled beneath their feet. The runes on the tree flared with light, and a low, rumbling growl echoed through the clearing. The air grew colder, and the whispers rose, filling the space with voices of the lost and the damned.

Evelyn's heart pounded as she watched Eldrin pour the elixir over the runes. The liquid hissed as it touched the bark, and a wave of green light pulsed from the tree, pushing back the darkness momentarily. But as the light faded, the ground around them erupted, and shadows surged forward, forming monstrous shapes that clawed at the group.

"Defend him!" Evelyn shouted, charging forward with Tristan and Lila at her side. Their weapons flashed as they fought back the shadows that lunged toward Eldrin.

The air was filled with the sound of clashing steel and the hiss of the shadows as they recoiled from the light of the fireflies. Evelyn's movements were swift and precise, her blade cutting through the darkness as she protected Eldrin. The tree groaned, its branches swaying as the runes pulsed faster, and the shadows became more aggressive, their claws reaching for the group.

Eldrin chanted, his voice merging with the whispers of the forest. The elixir's glow intensified, and the runes began to crack, green light spilling out from the fissures. But the shadows didn't relent, and Evelyn's muscles ached as she continued to fend off the onslaught.

Lila screamed as a shadow grabbed her leg, pulling her down. Evelyn turned, her heart racing, and sliced through the dark tendril, freeing Lila just in time. "Stay with me!" she shouted.

Eldrin's voice grew louder, his eyes glowing as he continued the incantation. "It's almost done—hold on!"

The shadows coalesced into a towering figure, its eyes blazing with an unnatural light. It lunged at Evelyn, its claws inches from her face. She raised her blade, deflecting the blow, but the force sent her stumbling back. Tristan rushed in, his sword clashing with the shadow as he pushed it away.

"We have to strike now!" Tristan yelled, his voice echoing through the chaos.

Eldrin's hands glowed with a bright light as he slammed his palm onto the tree. The runes shattered, and a wave of energy erupted, blasting the shadows back. The tree shook, its branches thrashing as the green light dimmed.

But as the light faded, Evelyn saw Eldrin stumble, his face pale. She rushed to his side. "Eldrin, are you okay?"

Eldrin shook his head, his expression pained. "I've used too much of my energy… but it's not enough." His eyes met hers, and there was a deep sadness in them. "The heart of the tree must be destroyed, and I'm the only one who can do it."

Evelyn's eyes widened. "What do you mean?"

Eldrin took a deep breath. "I have to bind my soul to the forest. It's the only way to sever the connection the ancient evil has with this place."

"No!" Evelyn grabbed his arm, her voice filled with desperation. "There has to be another way."

Eldrin smiled sadly. "There isn't. This is what I've prepared for all this time." He placed a hand on her shoulder. "You need to be strong. You have Lucian to save."

Tears welled up in Evelyn's eyes. "But I can't lose you."

Eldrin's voice was steady, filled with quiet resolve. "You won't. I'll be here—in the forest, in the fireflies. I'll watch over you."

As the shadows surged again, Eldrin chanted an incantation, his body glowing as he stepped toward the heart of the tree. The ground trembled, and the runes flared one last time. The shadows screamed, their forms twisting as they tried to stop him, but the light from Eldrin's soul grew brighter, pushing them back.

Evelyn watched, her heart breaking as Eldrin placed his hand on the tree's core. The light enveloped him, and the forest erupted in a blinding flash. The shadows let out a final, agonizing cry before dissolving into mist.

As the light faded, the tree began to wither, its branches turning to ash. The forest was still, the air warm and filled with the gentle glow of the fireflies.

Eldrin's form was gone, his essence merging with the light. Evelyn fell to her knees, tears streaming down her face as she whispered his name. The forest, now calm, seemed to echo with his voice, a whisper carried on the breeze.

Tristan and Lila stood beside her, their faces somber. Lila placed a hand on Evelyn's shoulder. "He gave us a chance."

Evelyn nodded, wiping her tears. "We have to honor him. We have to finish this."

The fireflies circled around them, their light a beacon of hope as they prepared for the final battle. Evelyn's heart ached with the loss of her friend, but she felt his presence in the light. Eldrin's sacrifice had weakened the ancient evil, and she knew they had one final fight ahead.

She stood, gripping her blade with renewed determination. "For Eldrin. For everyone who was lost. We end this."

The group moved forward, the fireflies guiding them through the forest, their light leading the way to the final confrontation. The ancient evil would fall, and Evelyn would not let Eldrin's sacrifice be in vain.

Chapter 41: "The Shadow's End"

The forest, now illuminated by the warm glow of the fireflies, felt different. The shadows no longer loomed as heavily, but a chill lingered in the air—a reminder that their task was not yet complete. Evelyn, Lila, and Tristan moved forward with determined steps, their minds fixed on the final stronghold where the ancient evil had retreated.

Eldrin's sacrifice hung heavy in the air, and each step Evelyn took felt like a weight she carried. The fireflies danced around them, their light growing stronger, as if guiding and protecting them, carrying Eldrin's presence. His last words echoed in her mind: I'll be here—in the forest, in the fireflies.

Lila's voice was soft, her eyes still wet. "Do you think he's really with us?"

Evelyn nodded, her voice steady despite the ache in her chest. "He is. And he gave us a chance. We have to make sure it counts."

Tristan's eyes were hard, his face set with grim determination. "For Eldrin, and for everyone the ancient evil has taken." He tightened his grip on his sword. "This ends today."

They pressed on, following the path illuminated by the fireflies. The forest seemed to open up, the trees parting to reveal a clearing unlike any they had seen before. In the center, a massive black stone altar rose from the ground, covered in pulsating veins of red and black energy. It was as if the ancient evil's lifeblood coursed through it.

Evelyn felt a shiver run down her spine. "This is it. The heart of the darkness."

The air around the altar was frigid, and the shadows that lingered in the clearing seemed to writhe as they approached, whispering threats and curses. The fireflies hovered in a protective circle around the group, their light pushing back the darkness.

Lila's hand tightened around her pendant. "How do we destroy it?"

Evelyn turned to Tristan, their eyes meeting in silent understanding. "We attack together. We sever its connection to the forest."

Tristan nodded, his face resolute. "The ancient evil will try to fight back. We have to be ready."

Evelyn took a deep breath, feeling the warmth of the fireflies around her. "Stay close. We move as one."

The three of them advanced, their weapons drawn, and as they neared the altar, the shadows erupted. Dark, spectral figures surged forward, their eyes glowing with a malevolent light. The ground trembled beneath their feet, and the air was filled with an unnatural chill.

Evelyn's heart pounded as she slashed at the shadows, her blade cutting through the darkness. The fireflies' light intensified, merging with each strike, pushing back the dark figures. Lila and Tristan fought beside her, their movements precise and swift as they defended against the onslaught.

The shadows hissed, their forms twisting and recoiling as the fireflies' light drove them back. Evelyn pushed forward, her gaze locked on the altar. "We have to reach it!"

Tristan deflected a shadow's attack, his sword flashing as he struck. "Keep going—I'll cover you!"

Lila moved with Evelyn, her eyes focused as she sliced through the shadows that lunged toward them. The fireflies formed a barrier around the two, their light merging into a bright halo that guided their path. As they neared the altar, the whispers grew louder, filling Evelyn's head with doubts and fears.

You will fail. You cannot defeat me.

Evelyn gritted her teeth, pushing the voice away. "We've come too far to turn back now!"

The shadows clawed at them, but the fireflies held their ground, their light growing stronger with every step. Evelyn reached the base of the altar, her eyes fixed on the pulsating veins of energy that snaked across its surface. She raised her blade, channeling her strength and the light that surrounded her.

Tristan and Lila fought off the remaining shadows, their faces set with determination as they defended her. "Do it, Evelyn!" Tristan shouted, his voice carrying over the roar of the shadows.

Evelyn's hands trembled, but she forced herself to steady her grip. She could feel the energy of the altar, the ancient evil's presence pulsing through it like a heartbeat. She raised her blade high, her eyes locking onto the heart of the darkness. "For Eldrin. For everyone."

She brought the blade down with all her strength, and as it struck the altar, a shockwave of energy erupted. The ground shook, and the shadows let out an ear-splitting scream as the fireflies' light intensified, merging with the energy of the blow. The altar cracked, fissures of light spreading across its surface as the ancient evil's power was severed.

The forest reacted violently, the trees thrashing as the ground trembled beneath them. The shadows writhed, their forms dissolving into mist as the fireflies' light burned through them. Evelyn felt the ancient evil's power weakening, its grip on the forest loosening.

But then, the air grew colder, and the shadows pulled back, coalescing into a single massive figure that rose from the altar. It loomed above them, its eyes burning with a fierce, unnatural light. It let out a roar that shook the air, and Evelyn felt the ground crack beneath her feet.

"Evelyn!" Lila screamed as the figure lunged forward.

Evelyn raised her blade, her eyes locked onto the creature. "We finish this—together!"

The fireflies surged, their light merging into a blinding glow that surrounded Evelyn, Lila, and Tristan. They charged as one, their weapons flashing as they struck at the creature. The air was filled with the sounds of clashing steel and the hissing screams of the ancient evil as it fought back.

Evelyn's blade glowed, and with every strike, she felt the power of the fireflies—of Eldrin's sacrifice—guiding her. The creature recoiled, its form flickering as the light burned through it. Lila and Tristan fought beside her, their movements in perfect sync as they attacked from every angle.

With a final, powerful strike, Evelyn plunged her blade into the creature's chest, and the light of the fireflies erupted in a blinding flash. The shadows screamed, their forms shattering into a burst of mist as the light consumed them. The ground shook, and the altar cracked completely, its veins of energy fading into nothingness.

The creature let out a final roar, its eyes wide with rage and fear, before it dissolved into the mist, leaving the clearing silent and still.

Evelyn fell to her knees, her breath coming in ragged gasps as the fireflies' light dimmed. The forest was quiet, the darkness receding as the ancient evil's presence vanished. The trees stood tall and still, their branches no longer twisted but strong and full of life.

Tristan and Lila joined her, their faces etched with exhaustion and relief. The fireflies hovered above them, their light soft and warm, a reminder of the sacrifice that had been made.

"It's over," Evelyn whispered, her voice barely audible.

Lila nodded, a tear sliding down her cheek. "Eldrin... he did it."

Tristan placed a hand on Evelyn's shoulder. "We all did. And we'll carry his memory with us."

Evelyn looked up, her eyes searching the forest. The fireflies danced above, their light merging with the dawn that began to break through the trees. She felt a sense of peace, a warmth that spread through her as she realized they had finally done it.

They had freed the forest.

As they stood together in the clearing, Evelyn felt a breeze rustle through the leaves, and for a moment, she could hear Eldrin's voice in the whispering wind. *You did well, Evelyn. Keep the light alive.*

She smiled, a tear slipping down her cheek. "Thank you, Eldrin."

The fireflies guided them back through the forest, their light a beacon of hope in the dawn. Evelyn knew their journey was far from over—there would always be darkness to fight, and there would always be light to protect.

But for now, she and her companions had won. And she carried the memory of those who had fallen, their light guiding her forward.

The forest was alive, and the shadows no longer held sway.

They were free.

Chapter 42: "Echoes of Light"

The forest was alive with the gentle hum of life. As the sun's rays filtered through the canopy, they painted the ground with patches of light and shadow, a reminder that the forest was now In balance. Evelyn, Lila, and Tristan walked quietly along the path, the fireflies' glow mingling with the warmth of the dawn. Each step felt lighter, the oppressive weight of darkness finally lifted.

Evelyn's eyes scanned the familiar trees, now free from their twisted forms, their branches strong and reaching toward the sky. The forest, once a place of nightmares, was transforming into a sanctuary of peace. She paused, listening to the breeze as it rustled through the leaves, and felt the presence of the forest's spirit—a warmth that had been absent for so long.

Lila and Tristan walked beside her, their expressions a mix of relief and exhaustion. Lila's eyes were bright as she looked around. "It feels so different now. It's like the forest is breathing again."

Evelyn nodded, a small smile touching her lips. "The darkness is gone. Eldrin's sacrifice made this possible."

Tristan's voice was soft but resolute. "He gave everything to free this place. We owe it to him to keep it safe."

The three of them continued, the fireflies hovering above like tiny guardians, their light guiding the way. They reached the grove where Eldrin had made his final stand. The ground was still marked by the battle—the remnants of shadows that had dissolved into the earth—but the light of the fireflies filled the space, transforming it into a place of reflection and memory.

Evelyn knelt, her fingers brushing the ground where Eldrin had fallen. She felt a pang of sorrow, the loss still fresh in her heart. "He's still with us," she whispered, her voice carried by the breeze. "He always will be."

Lila knelt beside her, placing a hand on Evelyn's shoulder. "He's part of the forest now, and he'll always guide us."

Tristan joined them, his gaze fixed on the fireflies swirling above. "We'll make sure his sacrifice wasn't in vain. The forest will become a sanctuary, and we'll protect it."

Evelyn stood, her eyes locking onto the path ahead. "We have work to do. The forest still needs healing, and we have to ensure it remains a place of balance."

As they continued through the grove, Evelyn felt the presence of Eldrin, the warmth of his sacrifice, in every firefly's glow. She knew they had not only defeated the ancient evil but had created something new—a place of light where darkness could no longer reign.

They made their way to the edge of the forest, where the trees opened up to reveal a view of the valley below. The sunlight stretched across the landscape, and the fireflies formed a spiral around the group, their light blending with the dawn. Evelyn felt a sense of peace settle over her. "This is the beginning of something new."

Lila and Tristan nodded, determination and hope filling their eyes. "We'll make this forest a place of light and safety," Lila said, her voice steady.

Tristan smiled. "And we'll find others who share our mission. We can build something lasting here."

Evelyn's gaze softened as she looked at her companions. "We've fought for this, and now we have a chance to create a future where the light will always shine."

As they turned back toward the forest, a figure emerged from the shadows—a man with dark hair and a familiar face. Evelyn's heart stopped for a moment as she recognized Lucian. He approached slowly, his expression hesitant but full of hope.

"Evelyn," he said, his voice filled with the weight of everything they had been through. "The forest led me back. I remember now... everything."

Evelyn's eyes filled with tears as she moved toward him. "Lucian... you're free."

Lucian nodded, his gaze meeting hers. "Eldrin's sacrifice gave me the strength to fight the darkness. And you... you never gave up on me."

Evelyn reached out, taking his hand. "I couldn't. I always believed there was something worth saving."

Lucian smiled, a tear sliding down his cheek. "I want to build a future with you. To make things right."

Evelyn's heart felt light as she nodded. "Then we do this together."

The fireflies surrounded them, their light a soft, glowing halo that wrapped them in warmth. Evelyn felt the presence of Eldrin in the gentle glow, a reminder that even in loss, there could be hope and renewal.

As they stood together, the fireflies' light brightened, merging with the sun's rays, casting long shadows that spoke of the journey they had taken and the future they would build. Evelyn knew that the forest would continue to heal and that she, Lucian, Lila, and Tristan would be its guardians—a new beginning forged from sacrifice and love.

The shadows had been defeated, and in their place, the light of the fireflies and the promise of a better future remained.

EPILOGUE: "A LIGHT That Never Fades"

YEARS PASSED, AND THE forest that was once shrouded in darkness became a sanctuary of life and light. Under the guidance of Evelyn, Lucian, Lila, and Tristan, the Guardians of the Fireflies, the woods flourished, becoming a haven for travelers, lost souls, and those seeking peace. The whispers that once filled the air with fear now carried the gentle echoes of hope, and the fireflies, ever watchful, led those who wandered safely through the forest's paths.

Evelyn stood at the heart of the forest one evening, her eyes scanning the familiar grove where Eldrin had given his life. The tree that once pulsed with dark energy was now covered in vibrant green leaves, its branches reaching toward the sky. Fireflies danced around it, their light mingling with the soft glow of the setting sun.

Lucian approached, his steps light as he joined her. "It's hard to believe this was once the center of all the darkness," he said quietly, his eyes reflecting the light of the fireflies.

Evelyn smiled, feeling a sense of peace that had been absent for so long. "We changed that. Eldrin's sacrifice gave us the strength to turn this place into something beautiful."

Lucian took her hand, his grip warm and reassuring. "And now, it's a place of light. A place where people can find solace."

As they stood together, the fireflies circled around them, their glow a reminder of all they had endured and the legacy they had built. Evelyn knew the journey they had taken had been filled with pain, loss, and sacrifice, but it had led them here—to a forest that now thrived because of the bonds they had formed and the battles they had fought.

Lila and Tristan joined them, smiles on their faces as they looked out at the landscape they had worked so hard to protect. "The forest is alive again," Lila said, her eyes bright with joy. "We did it."

Tristan nodded. "And we'll keep it this way. For Eldrin, for everyone."

Evelyn felt a warmth spread through her as she looked at her companions. The pain of the past was still there, but it had been transformed into a strength that bound them together. "The fireflies will guide us, just like they always have. And we'll continue to protect this forest, making it a place where darkness has no power."

As the sun dipped below the horizon, the forest came alive with the soft glow of the fireflies. Evelyn felt the presence of Eldrin in the light, his essence forever woven into the fabric of the woods he had fought to protect. She knew that as long as they stood as guardians, the forest would remain a beacon of hope, a place where light would always outshine the shadows.

Lucian squeezed her hand, and she smiled, feeling the future open up before them. "We have a lot of work to do, and a lot of lives to touch."

Together, they walked through the grove, their path illuminated by the fireflies that danced around them, their light guiding the way forward. The forest, now a place of renewal, was a testament to the power of love, sacrifice, and the unwavering strength of those who chose to fight for the light.

And as they moved deeper into the forest, the fireflies' glow shimmered, a promise that their light would never fade, no matter what shadows might come.

⌘

THE END.

⌘

THIS MARKS THE END of Evelyn's journey in Shadows of the Fireflies. Thank you for traveling through the shadows and light with her. I hope the fireflies' glow continues to light your path.

— Night Intruder

Don't miss out!

Visit the website below and you can sign up to receive emails whenever Night Intruder publishes a new book. There's no charge and no obligation.

https://books2read.com/r/B-A-GDRMC-XXDCF

BOOKS 2 READ

Connecting independent readers to independent writers.

Also by Night Intruder

Fading Ecoes
Fading Echoes: Stories Of Love And Loss Volume 1

Firefies Of The Heart
Shadows Of The Fireflies

Fireflies Of The Heart
Fireflies Of The Heart

Fragments of Grace and Dreams Book Of Poems Volume 1
Fragments of Grace and Dreams Book Of Poems Volume 1

Phantoms Breath
Phantom's Breath Volume 1
Phantom's Breath Elara's Veil Volume 2

About the Author

Writing under the pen name Night Intruder, the author weaves tales of mystery, darkness, and light. Fascinated by the supernatural and the power of the human spirit, they explore stories where love, sacrifice, and redemption collide in worlds both haunting and magical. When not writing, they are often lost in nature, drawing inspiration from the whispers of the woods and the dance of the fireflies.

Milton Keynes UK
Ingram Content Group UK Ltd.
UKHW032327221024
449917UK00004B/334

9 798227 544018